PRAISE FOR

BLISSFUL AND OTHER STORIES

"Steven Huff is a master storyteller in full command of his gifts, and *Blissful* is a cornucopia of marvelous and various Americana. Huff's fictions sometimes shock, never cheat, always instruct, and persist in the memory, as real as the best and worst days of our lives."
— STERLING WATSON, AUTHOR OF *SWEET DREAM BABY* AND *SUITCASE CITY*

"Steven Huff is a master stylist and an American original. He has traveled the winding roads to the base of the human heart, mapping them through every strange and delirious curve. What a pleasure to be along for the ride."
— JEDEDIAH BERRY, AUTHOR OF *THE MANUAL OF DETECTION*

"Huff's characters occupy the edges, the rich ecotones between city and rural, wealthy and poor, native and wandering, needy and full. They are also buffeted by the fates, living and dying not by chance but as organized by some all-seeing, -knowing, -powerful hand with a sardonic sense of irony and humor."
--STEPHEN LEWANDOWSKI, AUTHOR OF *UNDER FOOT*

BLISSFUL

AND OTHER STORIES

OTHER BOOKS BY STEVEN HUFF

FICTION
Pig in Paris

POETRY
The Water We Came From
More Daring Escapes
A Fire in The Hill

NONFICTION
Knowing Knott: Essays on
an American Poet (editor)

BLISSFUL

AND OTHER STORIES

STEVEN HUFF

ROCHESTER, NY

Back cover art and illustrations by Fawndolyn Valentine
Front cover and book design by Nina Alvarez

For permission to reprint portions of this book,
or to order a review copy, contact:
Editor@CosmographiaBooks.com

ISBN-13: 978-0692944264 (Cosmographia Books)
ISBN-10: 0692944265

For Betsy

Stories

After heaven crashed I dove in the river,
retrieved the black box & pried it open.
I know it was none of my business.

LIFE IS BRIEF

Later that day, someone would claim to have seen a surface-to-air missile strike the plane. Another witness on the ground would claim two or three missiles, he couldn't be sure. But they were disregarded because, if such a weapon had hit Flight 371 while flying over farm country, where would it have come from? Besides, it was snowing hard and the plane was above the clouds, and investigators doubted anyone could have seen the aircraft from the ground.

The captain had been talking to the control tower at Buffalo International about runway conditions when the aircraft disappeared from radar and crashed into a field of frozen corn stubble in New York State, fourteen miles north of the Pennsylvania border, raising such an enormous cloud of smoke and dirt and snow that some locals thought an asteroid had struck. The actual cause of the crash would not be made public for several days: a homemade bomb mailed as a prank by two geeky Cincinnati boys, and meant to go off in the girls' dormitory of a little private college near Syracuse where the sister of one of them was studying piano. It was meant to smoke and stink up the place and drive the girls out into the snow in their underwear, not to bring down a plane. Yet, even after that discovery, the missile theory persisted on talk radio.

Madeleine Weeks had boarded the flight at Minneapolis about one o'clock that morning. The day before, slouched at a desk in a St. Cloud bungalow where she was house-sitting, she'd called a travel agent and booked a ticket after trying for hours to figure out where Attica Prison actually was, and after realizing there was no commercial airport anywhere near the place, trying to decide what city was closest. Must be Buffalo, and she even rode her bicycle into town in the ten degree weather, wearing a snowsuit she'd found in a closet, to hand the agent the Visa card she'd found in a box in the back of a desk drawer in the owner's office room for a furiously fast trip—one day up and the next day back. She figured if she heaped Howlin' Wolf's dog-dish with enough Ken-L-Ration and filled his water bowl to the brim, and cleaned up all the poop and piss when she got back thirty-six hours later, there'd be no harm done and the owners of the house would be none the wiser. Provided Wolf didn't chew the hell out of the couch while she was gone. She had to go. She didn't know how not to go. What's the big hurry? the agent had asked. Life is brief, Madeleine Weeks replied.

After boarding she dozed in her seat until she felt the plane jolt into motion. As it picked up speed her eyes skimmed the frozen runway concrete the way she used to drag a finger in the water when she'd ridden in her father's motorboat as a child. No changing her mind now, the plane was lifting off. She slumbered back into her dreams.

It stopped in Cincinnati around 3:30 a.m. Snow was falling hard, and it kept the plane on the ground for more than two-and-a-half hours during which time the captain kept promising they were about to take off and forbidding anyone to get out of their seats. When they were finally airborne again, Madeleine's bladder felt like it would burst like the balloons she used to fill from a faucet when she was a girl, filling and filling until they exploded and soaked everyone dumb enough to stand too close. The plane hit turbulence, banging up and down like the universe was about to split its seams. When the captain gave the word to unbuckle, a mad dash for the toilets ensued by half the people on board. Madeleine waited in line while the plane shook sadistically.

"You waiting too?" asked the woman standing behind her, apparently hoping some of the people in line were just standing there for the excitement, and would soon sit down and leave the woman a clear path to the pot.

"Of course," Madeleine snapped. She regretted it

momentarily then remembered she wasn't a nun anymore. No more Sister Clara, no more Sister Nice-guy. She could snap now like a bear trap if she wanted.

"Sorry," said the woman.

"It's all right. They never put enough toilets on airplanes." Actually she wasn't sure this was true, since she'd been on a plane only a few times in her life, shuttled off to relatives when she was a girl so her parents could take vacations. This was her first adult flight, since nuns don't fly much.

"What do you do?" the woman asked, and Madeleine thought that was a startling question given that almost nothing mattered now except pissing. But she realized that the woman was simply trying to be friendly, grace under pressure.

"I'm a professional house-sitter."

"I'm a nurse."

"Really. I was a nurse once." A nun RN, actually, as well as a choir director, and a counselor, and a janitor on Tuesdays, and the Thursday-through-Sunday breakfast cook.

"I'm on my way to my cousin's funeral in Buffalo."

Now Madeleine turned around and looked at the woman who was a good three inches shorter, a bit of a tub, actually. Most of the sisters Madeleine had lived with had turned into tubs exactly like the shape of this little woman. They liked to eat, those girls. Not that Madeleine didn't, but she'd always been wired a little hot, had stayed lean, and had gotten out while her hair was still red.

"Sorry to hear that."

"I never liked him. Beat me up all the time when we were kids. But I'm still sorry he's dead."

The plane shook so violently that little screams came from the coach seats. Followed by another great shake. Children cried. The captain's voice came on again. A little turbulence, he said, I'm going to have to ask everyone to take your seat again. Or words to that effect. But no one was going anywhere. Let the damned plane shake its wings off.

"Do we really have to sit down?" asked the woman.

"If you don't want to piss your pants you'd better keep your place in line."

"I can't hold it like I used to."

"Me neither."

"Where are you going?" the woman asked.

Madeleine knew that question was coming. But she didn't have an answer she could say out loud. She couldn't say, I'm going to meet an inmate at Attica Prison. He's getting out this morning at 10 o'clock and I'm going to meet him there. I used to visit him when he was at Sing Sing when I lived down that way. But the last time I went he'd been transferred the night before to Attica and he had no way of letting me know. So I sat there for hours waiting before somebody bothered to tell me he was gone to Attica. He's a gentle beast, a little like an ox, maybe. Oh yeah, and he's older than me, too, by a decade at least. I've fallen in love and I've decided to marry him. Now, don't get me wrong, you fat little puppy, I didn't come to this decision lightly. I've thought about it, I've sat up till dawn some nights thinking about it. And yes, I've prayed. God still does listen to me, even if I ran away from Him. Anyway, I'm going. What plans? You mean like, when we're going to tie the knot, where we're going to live? Well, I'm going to fly him back to St. Cloud. Then maybe we'll head south where he's got people. Or maybe we'll just go someplace and screw.

A few more shakes and the captain begged people to sit. Flight attendants pleaded with them.

When the woman realized Madeleine wasn't going to answer her question, she said, "This is my first time on a plane. Funny, it would take my nephew's death to get me up in the air. Though I never knew it would be so scary. Are flights usually like this?"

But Madeleine barely heard her.

How do I know he's really getting out this morning? Another good question I couldn't answer if the snoopy little bitch asked. Yes, I know how prison administration can jerk you around. They could say, Whoops, we gotta keep him another six weeks. But according to him, he's maxing out, meaning he's done his whole twenty years and a few months, and flunked all his parole hearings that could have gotten him out earlier. So, maybe he's been a behavior problem in the pen. Maybe he's one of those guys that I've read about who throw shit through the bars of their cells at the guards when they're delivering dinners. That's usually a sign of intelligence in kids, I don't know what it means at his age. What's he going to do for a job when he gets out? I'll be damned if I know. Is he going to house-sit with me? Are you out of your mind? When I marry him my house-sitting days are baked and burnt. We're going to rent a house somewhere and sit there and figure out what the hell to do.

With the next big shake the woman behind Madeleine was in tears, hanging onto the back of a seat. Some children were crying. The line was moving so slowly that Madeleine suspected people of dallying in the toilet, painting fingernails and checking make up, and so forth.

"Are we going to die?" asked the woman. "Level with me."

"Not before you pee, I don't think," Madeleine answered.

The woman laughed. Madeleine would have laughed too, but it might have made her piss her pants.

"What's his name?" the woman asked.

Huh? Madeleine thought, did I just do all my thinking out loud? "What did you ask?"

"I asked, what's his name? I figure there must be a man at the end of your trip."

"Albert," she said. Buick Albert Carr. His father had thought Buick was a cool name to go with Carr, but as soon as the old man disappeared from the family, Buick began calling himself by his middle name. At least, that's how he told the story to her.

At last it was Madeleine's turn. A couple years back, when she was still Sister Clara, she would have let the poor woman behind her go first. But not now. In the stall she dropped her jeans and yanked down her panties and sat down heavily on the sticky seat. She'd held it so long she didn't know if she could let go of it now. She took a deep breath.

A great boom happened beneath her, deep in the cargo hold of the plane. Holy God. Yes, an explosion, loud as a freight train hitting a bulldozer at a crossing, and she had just enough moment to wonder what it was when another boom followed so loud it was visible, a shaking rainbow of lights. She heard shrieks outside the bathroom door, then she heard nothing. She was being sucked down the toilet, as if nature's Hoover had her in its vacuum.

Now she was out in the air, somewhere over America, her legs above her head, her jeans and panties around her ankles, and her purse floating as if flung in a moment of ecstasy. She was above the snow clouds, and if she had remained conscious she would have thought they looked as though she could walk across them—like a vision she'd had as a child of the road to heaven that she'd walk someday if she finished her life faithfully as a nun. But in fact now she was falling through those clouds some three quarters of a mile west of a great blue chunk of falling ice that was the chemical concoction of excrement that had burst from the plane's septic holding tank when the explosion had occurred, and which had, like her, frozen almost instantly in the high altitude. In fact, her last thought was frozen on her brain the way the outline of a breath freezes on a window, and the thought was, *Albert will never believe this. Albert will never—*

ZIGROVIOFF

I wanted to be Zigrovioff, the man who turned the big iron wheel that opened the floodgate of the dam on rainy days. It emptied river water over spillways, regulating the water level in the canal, which intersected with the river above the dam. In dry spells, he closed the gate and raised the river. I mean, it would have been a good life if I was Zigrovioff, if operating the floodgate was what being Zigrovioff meant. But only Zigrovioff could be Zigrovioff. And I knew this. He was bald and muscular and smoked a cigarette while he turned the wheel. He had no measuring stick, he just knew the river. Sometimes it rose because of a rainstorm a hundred miles upstream. Another pair of eyes wouldn't see the river changing. But Zigrovioff would be at the wheel, turning it like he was steering a ship. His muscles straining the seams of his shirt.

I was the neighbor boy who snuck into his house when he was at work and his wife, Gloria, was out driving somewhere. I went through their drawers looking at their personal things. I was otherwise a good boy, a good student;

I do not know what my fascination was with their house and their private stuff. But this went on for a couple years, and it amazes me now to think that I never got caught. I went in their back door—which they never locked—in broad daylight.

I left only the smallest signs of myself. For example, I took the Vaseline Petroleum Jelly out of their medicine cabinet and put it in the fridge, then took the blueberry jelly out of the fridge and put it in the medicine cabinet. Things like that. And I suppose they made Zigrovioff shrug and put things back where they belonged. But a few times they led to confused arguments between Zigrovioff and Gloria. I could hear them from our backyard two doors away.

And I always left with a memento: a bottle opener, a pair of Gloria's panty hose, a ruler, a fountain pen, a condom, a bullet from the chamber of a loaded pistol that I found in their nightstand. Never anything of great value. I never took any jewelry or money, though I found plenty of both. Yet, what I took were things I thought they would miss. There was a removable grate in the wall of my bedroom, and I stuffed it all in there, in the wall.

Gloria was beautiful, at least to my young eyes. Once in a while on a still summer evening I'd hear her holler, "*Ha!*" enormously loud, both lungs at full bore. This would be followed by some other sharp chatter that I could not make out. They became familiar sounds. But her *"Ha"* never sounded like it was meant to be funny. More like a taunt. Zigrovioff's voice from a distance sounded like hard things cracking together, like billiard balls. As their arguments progressed, her voice became sharp and splintering, like a china bowl dropped on the patio.

I imagined them arguing about the disappearance of a monogram washcloth. Her scarlet G-string. I saw him sitting in a lawn chair listening to her blister him with accusations, a bottle of whiskey lying on its side on a table, and he finally picking up the pistol, his face contorted with hatred. And Gloria hollering, *"Ha!"* He takes aim, he knows this means the end of his life as well as hers, but in his rage and delirium it all makes sense. He pulls the trigger, but the hammer falls on the empty chamber, the one I had taken the bullet from. In their shock, they come to their senses. "Aw Jesus, Gloria, I'm sorry. Forgive me." Her face is white as a golf ball. "Oh, Zigrovioff," she says. Then they get into an argument about the gun: where did the other bullet go, he wants to know. He accuses her of firing the gun somewhere. "What the hell were you shooting at, rats?" "If I wanted to shoot a rat, I'd shoot you," she hollers.

Sometimes, after I'd heard an argument over their fence, I would see Zigrovioff driving off as the sun was setting, and I would wonder if he had Gloria in the trunk, if he was going to throw her through the floodgate, let her slide down the spillway into the lower river. In fact, she died of lung cancer while I was away at college. My mother told me about it when I came home for the holidays. "She went fast," she said.

And for a long time I sat on the side of my bed, realizing that I had a dead woman's G-string, pantyhose, and other personal stuff in the wall of my room. Why was it there? Why was I here?

One summer evening when I was paddling a canoe with Anne, my girlfriend, we came to the dam and I saw Zigrovioff on its pinnacle, his shirt off, a cigarette in his mouth, turning the wheel. He looked tanned and strong. It was a brutally hot night, the city was dry as dust. I waved to him. He waved back without taking his attention off the wheel. He was accustomed to chummy boaters coming by and distracting him.

"Oh," Anne said, "that man."

"You know my neighbor?"

She glowered. "My brother used to mow his lawn. Until one day when he showed up, he grabbed him by the shirt and started slapping him. Accused him of stealing stuff out of his house. What bullshit."

"So, he's a brute," I said. And we paddled away.

I never really knew Zigrovioff. One night I was in Bud's, a bar near our street, and he came in and sat next to me and threw down several shots and beer chasers, all the while arguing with a man a couple stools away. I couldn't understand what it was about, but two women's names came up, and when they started to shove each other the bartender told them to take it outside. Zigrovioff grunted and took off his shirt, and followed the other man out the back door. We went outside and watched the two men in the alley circling each other, occasionally landing a punch. It wasn't much of a fight.

I went inside, and saw his shirt hanging over a chair. I put it on over my t-shirt, and sat at the bar. It was a green short sleeve, and smelled like him, a scent I remembered lurking in his house. When the two men and the spectators came in, I was sitting at the bar drinking a beer.

"Where the hell is my shirt?" Zigrovioff hollered. "Who took my goddamned shirt?"

The other man had a bloody nose, and held a handkerchief against his nostrils.

There was a pack of Chesterfields in the breast pocket, and I lit one. Zigrovioff sat at the bar and goddamned everything on earth. Someone pointed at the shirt I was wearing. He looked at it and said, "Naw, that ain't it." And he eventually drove home in his t-shirt.

I ordered another beer, and I asked for a shot.

FIDDLE

My job was to swallow twenty-thousand milligrams of vitamin C every morning, wash it down with half a gallon of orange juice along with a cocktail glass of other supplements, crazy stuff like bee pollen, gingko leaf. Whatever city we happened to be in, the band's manager located a sauna where I sat the better part of the day, drinking distilled water and chicken broth, sweating disgusting puddles, and gobbling down more of those damned vitamins. Around eight o'clock, Frankie's driver swung by my hotel and drove me to the concert hall, where I was ushered in and seated behind the stage in a sound booth. Usually Frankie himself would stop on his way to his dressing room and slap me on the back. He'd say. "Be good tonight, Fiddle." Or when he was particularly rattled, it was, "Be perfect. You hear me?"

We'd do the sound check. And the crew would hook up a closed circuit TV so I could see the boys. I had to see their mouths close up. Some warm-up band would be on first and I'd practice zeroing in on those younger rockers to get a feel for the stage and the acoustics before my boys came on.

They put me in that damned booth because one of the boys had a bad cold, and I had to sing his part. I'd get the *go* signal, I'd yank the mike to my lips, my fingers sweating so much vitamin C that they glistened yellow. The stage filled up with soft light like an aquarium, and the four came swinging on stage with the long, Oooooo-ooeeh-ooooooh-ooooh about the rag doll girl, hands-down the sweetest harmony in rock 'n' roll history. That winter one of the boys always had the sniffles if not laryngitis. They passed it one to another like the clap. But I knew their parts, I knew their vocal ranges. All Frankie or Tommy or Bobby or Nicky had to do was open his mouth, and I filled in the part smooth as satin bed sheets. I was the one who couldn't catch cold, no matter what.

I didn't hang around after a concert. I'd flag a cab back to my hotel nerved and exhausted and I'd strip off my clothes and take a hot shower, then sit on my bed and try to meditate on the wallpaper pattern until those adolescent lyrics were out of my head: *Big girls don't cry, Sherry, Sherry baby*. Sometimes I had to follow up with a colonic irrigation. Anything to get out the static. Because, if that didn't work I'd be in a bar throwing down shots like swatting flies.

Then Frankie would call me at six in the morning and scald my ass for some little slip. "You know what would happen to me if somebody caught on to this shit? You know what would happen to The Four Seasons?"

He'd say, "I'm gonna come over there and kick your skinny ass." Then the *oh-yeah* stuff, and *you just try it.* He'd say, "I'm gonna have your legs busted for Christmas," and then I was gonna kick his mother's ass, and he was gonna kick my mother's butt. He was always going to send somebody over to my room to beat me up. I realized later that he was bluffing: he never had a goon on the payroll. But back then I was shaking.

Once and only once I told him, "You know what rubs you so raw? If I can do your voice so spot on, it must mean you're not God's answer to music after all."

He went loony, and he had such a bad cold, his voice sounded like worn-out break shoes. Ten minutes later there was a knock on my door and I thought it was the guy who was supposed to bust my legs, and I threw it open and grabbed this bellhop by the lapels and made his eyes bug out. Poor kid was only trying to deliver my breakfast. It was a tough job, I'm telling you, but it paid top bucks because there wasn't another mouth in the whole USA that could ape any rock 'n' roller's voice. I mean anybody's. Just me.

Then one morning Frankie used the "H" word. Called me a hillbilly. And I quit. Any man in his right shoes would have done the same.

I'm probably the only piss ant from Loeb Hill, Arkansas who ever wore a pair of six hundred dollar Guccis. I wore a busted pair of my daddy's shoes to my first job, a little hog's ass radio station where my job was to spin records, filling in for the regular guy who was off on drunken sprees half the time. But I started telling jokes and working impersonations into my program. I had Ferlin Husky and Hank Williams down flat. My handle was Billy "Fiddlehead" Walker. Later it was just Fiddlehead. Or if you met me in a bar it was plain Fiddle.

One afternoon, in the spring of '49, the Matthews brothers of the Foggy River Boys were driving through Arkansas and happened to tune into WLHR, Loeb Hill Radio, and caught one of my routines where I did Roy Acuff and Ernie Tubb arguing about which one was going take some girl out for a hotdog, and it was probably a little too suggestive for its time, but the Matthews boys started to howl so hard they had to pull the car over to the roadside and wipe their eyes. Then they sat there and listened to me sing a few bars of "Honkytonk Angel," throwing in my own happy lyrics. And it just so happened that Monty Matthews was suffering from laryngitis and blowing snot, and one of them got the big idea that I could fill in for him. Fill in how? Well, maybe we could put him behind the curtain with a mike and let him sing Monty's parts. So, this '49 Cadillac pulls up in front of the station and these cowboy hats climbed out.

All someone had to do was sneeze around The Foggy River Boys, and at least one of them would be running a fever the next morning. So I had regular work for about as long as I wanted. Some of the members wandered off in the coming years and were replaced by other singers that also caught colds, while I stood out of sight, singing anybody's part that couldn't do it himself. People didn't believe in vitamins so much in those days, and they'd never heard of a sauna, so my time off was my own, more or less. Well, my Foggy River friends became The Jordanaires, and a few years later they became the backup singers for Elvis. If you saw him on that legendary segment of "The Ed Sullivan Show" in '56, I'm singing for the short guy, second from the left, when the King blasts into his performance of "Hound Dog." That was also the first time I got put in a real sound booth, first time I had headphones on. The audience was going rank nuts, and if I got off the harmony part a bit no one in the universe would know. But, fact was, I stayed pretty tight.

So Elvis comes backstage afterward and says, "You're

gonna call your momma now." I must have given him a funny look, because he says, "Fiddle, I'm gonna put a shoe right up your ass if you don't pick up that phone over there. Have some respect." Elvis wore regular Thom McAn shoes himself. But this was long before the cape and the ruby-studded belt and girdle.

I was pulling in dough with a squeegee while I worked for the King and The Jordanaires. I had a turquoise Buick and white bucks, a gold string tie, my own house in Memphis. And I found a couple rich women who were probably fifteen years older than me, too old for Elvis I figured, because I was sick of him walking off with my dates. By winter of '62, I was tired of the same old songs, and I'd finally fallen out with the King after he strolled right into my house and lured my dinner companion away in his pink El Dorado. On his way out of the house with my date—who was his date now, and he didn't care how old she was—he saw Jerry Lee Lewis on my TV, pounding the keys. He said, "You go on ahead, honey, I'll be right out." He watched her through the door curtain, and when she was in the car he pulled a Beretta and fired a single shot dead through the center of the screen, Jerry Lee vanishing in a great ball of smoke and glass fragments. Burnt-circuit stink. Everything in my brain stopped, along with my breath, as if the bullet had gone through me. It's well-known that he liked to shoot televisions, and I knew that the next day men would deliver a bigger TV, compliments of the King. But at this moment, he turned and look at me, that curled-lip smile he had. I had just been put in my place.

So I was ready to go when Frankie hired me away. I also did occasional gigs for the Beach Boys, Bobby Vinton, and Smokey Robinson. I even did Cher one time. I was a long way from Loeb Hill. But soon my age stalked me. Vocal cords commonly stretch and hang like slack suspenders, but I worked hard to keep mine tight, my voice young. I mean, I worked goddamned hard.

I was in a bad section of Memphis in a bar called Clammy's, where I hung out after I left the Seasons, drank gin by the quart and tried to face up to the fact that I was the greatest super-talented nobody that ever lived. If I told people what I used to do for a living they'd roll their eyes and walk away. Once in a while I'd get on a payphone and call Elvis up where he was living in that ridiculous mansion, his life barren as Pluto's moon, and sing, "'Are you lonesome tonight...'" But my funds were dwindling. My Buick was rusting in my driveway. I wondered how I was going to keep the lights on in my house and still throw back the Beefeater. The bartender handed me the phone.

"Fiddle," came Frankie's voice. He knew right where

to find me. "Look, there's a problem here. Frankie's got a bad cold."

And I'm thinking, is this guy off his nut, talking about himself in the third person?

"I don't get it," I said.

"No, no, not me," he said. "I wouldn't touch you again with a bull whip. I'm talking about Sinatra. He's got the Hollywood Bowl tomorrow, the biggest gig in town. I told him you're the man. And he said to get your ass on a plane." Those Jerzy boys stick together. "There's a big fifty in it for you."

I said I didn't have funds enough for a rocking horse ride.

"Fiddle. You blockheaded hillbilly. There's a ticket waiting for you at the airport."

A few minutes later a limousine pulls up to that sleazy bar. I thought I had left the world of illusion behind. Now, on my way to the airport, I realized that phantasm has its dark angels, and that they'd come for one of their lost sheep.

Next day I walked into a big plush office in Hollywood, and there sits Ol' Blue Eyes at a long table with a tumbler of scotch, his hair all messed up, and enough bottles of cough syrup to put a whole orchestra to sleep. And blond babes handing him silk snot rags.

"You're Fiddle?" he croaked. I saw a fleeting look of

fear and agony in his eyes. Then he poked a thumb over his shoulder. "Get your ass in the back room."

The same women set me up in this little closet space with headphones and a dozen Sinatra albums. But I didn't need them. I knew the songs by heart. I played them all the time for those superannuated girlfriends that I used to have.

That night some quack shot Blue Eyes full of steroids and a bouquet of amphetamines. He was a walking chemical garden, and he strolled out on that stage like an Archangel. The band was perfect. I knew some of those guys, they were in Bobby Darin's band when I did a couple gigs for him—back in the day.

My sound booth was down in a damp basement that reeked of Pine Sol. The first hour of the concert was a beauty. "Strangers in the Night," "That Old Black Magic," the whole ring-a-ding thing. The audience was weeping with joy, my voice felt like sweet milk in my throat, and I was having a fine time.

At intermission there was a knock on the door of the sound booth. I thought it was going to be Sinatra to pat me on the back and slip me a couple extra big ones. It was the stage manager, looking like a specter from hell. "Nancy's got a cold," he said.

"Huh, what're you talking about?"

"Nancy Sinatra, mutton head. She's singing that duet, 'Something Stupid,' with her dad in about five minutes. You're gonna have to do both of them, in harmony. Sorry, champ." And he walked away.

"Wait, wait," I hollered down the hall after him. "Can't you find the record or something?"

I still get a knot in my guts when I smell Pine Sol.

I did my hyperventilated best at something I'd never done before, trying to blend two voices with one mouth. It came off sounding like Jimmy Durante singing a duet with a mina bird. I couldn't see the audience on the TV, but I didn't need to. The disaster was all over the old man's face—and Nancy's. After his encore, I bolted down the hallways trying to find an exit, but I was a rat in a maze. It took four of his goons to pin me down.

I have to say, there was a benevolent side to Sinatra. I still got my fifty grand. A deal is a deal in his world. And I got use of an ocean-side chalet, all-expenses paid, with a nurse and a house servant and all the single-malt scotch I could put away while my legs healed. But one day I'm on the back deck in my wheelchair waiting for breakfast and a shadow fell over me. I look up and there's these two brush cuts in black suits. Whatever this was about, I figured I was dead. I said, "You come to autograph my cast?"

The brush cut on the right said, "Nixon's got laryngitis."

"Is that the biggest problem he's got?"

His face was like dry ice. "He has to announce his resignation tonight on TV. Mr. Sinatra said you're the man. And to get your ass on a plane."

I started to sweat. I said, "What's in it for me?"

One brush cut looked at the other then said, "Did you know the IRS is looking for you?"

They pushed my wheelchair through the chalet and out the front door where two women who were also in black suits stood beside a silver van. I recognized them as the girls who fed the fancy snot rags to Sinatra. One of them opened the back door of the vehicle and the two brush cuts hoisted me in, chair and all, and the girls chocked my wheels. Then the whole bunch of us were on our way to LAX where, I gathered, Air Force One was being refueled.

I smiled at the two women, and I said, "*I am not a crook.*"

"Shut the hell up," said the brush cut who was driving.

"I have to practice. *Let others wallow in Watergate.*"

"I said shut up," as he rolled to a stop at a red light.

I said, "*You won't have me to kick around anymore.*" And I grabbed for the back door latch. I was going to launch my chair into the street. But the silk hanky girls got me by my neck. One of them held a needle, and yanked up my sleeve. The other stuck a gun in my ear.

She said, "Take your vitamins like a good boy."

LIGHTNING

They'd dressed up for the wedding, sort of. Terry Kedsell wore his brown, corduroy sport jacket, though the weather was snowy and he would have been better off in his winter coat. And she in the lacey, delicate, off-white dress she'd worn to other people's nuptials so many times that threads frayed along the seams and hem. And a thin, un-matching blue overcoat. Two people in their forties, never before married, who had always watched other people take that step, ate and drank at their weddings and wondered what it was like, how it might feel immediately after taking the vows. She was keeping the name that she had signed on the license, Dominica Morley. She was Norwegian-Scotch-Irish-English-Welsh on her father's side and Italian on her mother's, and her mother had won the name game when she was born. But everyone, even her mother, had always called her Sunday.

Now as they drove home from the courthouse he realized that Sunday was really his. Or, sort of. In that dress, in her pale white hose, in her woven fabric shoes.

And he hoped she was as aroused as he was, because he was thinking about taking those things off of her piece by piece. The signs were good: she was laughing about the clumsy ceremony, how the judge had spun on his heel and walked away when it was over, and didn't even shake their hands. How Johnny Fish and his cousin Dorie, who stood up for them, had dressed up better than they had themselves, so that the waitress in the bar they went to for lunch thought that their two Seneca Indian friends were the actual bride and groom.

But he knew he was marrying into trouble because he'd known her long enough to see that the way she lived was like driving a car on ice with no seatbelts. Not because she wanted it that way, he was sure that she didn't. But the best cards that she ever drew were like four of diamonds, five of clubs, Go directly to jail. Do not pass GO, do not collect $200, etc. Actually, she'd been in jail once, for a weekend. And the little café she'd inherited from her mother was hanging by a thread, no matter how hard she worked.

On the porch steps to the house he picked her up to carry her in.

She said, "Knock it off, Kedsell. Your back is about as good as—"

But he didn't put her down.

Sunday said, "The fucking door, Kedsell. How are you

gonna unlock it without dropping me on the porch?"

"Reach in my left pocket. Keys are there."

Inside he staggered with her in his arms and finally made it to the couch where she landed hard on the cushions. Then he straightened up and unbuttoned his sport coat. For a moment he couldn't read her face: was she suddenly afraid of him standing over her? Then she looked at his shoes.

"Dorie said, if you've got oversized feet, it means you're gonna grow bigger. Another way that a man is like a puppy." Then she cracked up.

Kedsell asked her if she wanted more champagne. They'd drank one bottle in the car in the parking lot of the courthouse with Dorie and Johnny, passing it back and forth, bubbling over on their shoes.

"I've got to go to work," she said. Then she looked at her watch. "Okay, I've got a little bit yet."

She went into the bedroom and came out minutes later in black jeans, a sweater and sneakers, her usual work attire. He popped the cork and it bounced off the kitchen ceiling and landed in the open butter dish with a soft splat. They both stared at the cork for a few seconds as if they expected it to say something. He poured the champagne into the two crystal flutes that Dorie had given them. They sat and drank it and looked at each other over the table.

One thing he knew for sure, he hadn't married the same woman he knew years ago. And yet he had. And she was, and wasn't. Because sometimes it seemed that another woman had slipped into her skin somewhere along the way with all new revelations of behavior. But the old Sunday kept showing up, the way old wallpaper flowers sometimes assert their faces through the paint that was meant to cover them. Like the t-shirt he found once in the bottom of her drawer when she sent him there to find her KY jelly, with the printed slogan *Keep your dirty hands off*, and a picture of a woman kicking a man in the crotch. It seemed to bite at him. He'd married a woman behind a woman behind another woman, and on and on back, though he'd only exchanged rings with the woman in the front of that line.

Twenty years before, it was Donovan Hickey that Sunday was in love with, not Kedsell. She never moved in with Donovan, though he tried like hell, bought furniture that she liked, painted his living room walls a luminous orange at her mere suggestion that it might look interesting. But Sunday was only twenty-two then and probably didn't want to think about long-range consequences. The sorting-out process that brought him and Sunday together finally in their early middle-age was blurry, almost untraceable. Each of them had been in love with this one and that one, and made some forever promises. Furniture was bought and dumped, walls repainted, rings thrown out of car windows at high speed. All of their relationships had a way of breaking up right before Christmas, as if they wanted to avoid having to buy an expensive present.

One fiery August afternoon Sunday and Donovan and Jumpy and Kedsell had decided to get some friends together to skinny dip at Hilford State Park, near the Big Tree Reservation. This was when Sunday was still balling Donovan—long ago. Dorie went along that day, and Johnny Fish, among others. Everyone was drinking beer and somebody brought sloe gin, and somebody else brought a couple giant steaks to barbecue afterward, although no one remembered to bring a grill or even charcoal.

Bear Pond was the most secluded water in the park, more or less off limits. You had to drive down an access trail that was just wide enough for the wheelbase of Kedsell's car. Donovan drove behind him in his jeep. Mosquitos were horrendous, but once they were in the water and thoroughly wet, they weren't so bad. Besides, in an hour they were drunk.

That was the first time Kedsell saw Sunday without clothes. She had a lightning-like scar down her back, red from the top of her right shoulder to the left cheek of her butt. Everybody was hushed about it for some reason.

When he asked Dorie what caused it, she said, "That . . . we don't talk about." So it was another couple years before Donovan himself gave Kedsell a version when they were drinking in the Leghorn Lounge south of Hilford. Donovan was drinking bourbon that night and snarling like a peevish mutt—he was pissed off about losing Sunday to some other character, which had happened about a week before. Anyway, Kedsell asked him about the scar.

"You telling me you don't know that?" Donovan said.

"Would I be asking you if I did?"

Donovan sucked back his cigarette and studied the ceiling for a minute or two. He blew a stream of smoke straight in the air. "All right, are you ready for this? One rainy afternoon when Sunday was seventeen, she was balling this guy named Alfieri in her bedroom in her parents' house. It was a hot day even though it was raining and they had the window open. I don't know where the hell her parents were at the time. But I think it was after her father ran off. Anyway, are you ready for this? She was on top, riding Alfieri like a porpoise, when this bolt of lightning came through the window and put the white sword right through her back. Left that big jagged scar, and it fried Alfieri right between her legs."

Kedsell sputtered, "Come on."

Donovan's nostrils flared, "You think I'm making this

up? She said smoke even came out of Alfieri's nose."

Kedsell said no, he didn't mean to say that Donovan, who was sometimes called Mellow for the Donovan song "Mellow Yellow" (which was ridiculous because he was almost never mellow), was fabricating. But he really wasn't sure. How could she have survived such a thing? And if she did, how could she ever be normal again? And wasn't she more or less normal, at least on a subjective scale? Who wouldn't end up in the nut house over something like that? And probably never come out again.

"How come I never heard this before?"

Donovan rocked forward and crushed his cigarette out in the ashtray like he was mashing a bug. "That was when you was in the army, pecker-head. Besides, both families hushed up the exact circumstances. How would you like to be Alfieri's mother and have to overhear somebody making a joke about how her son died? Huh?"

By that point, Donovan was beginning to take on the snake face he wore when he was getting pissy drunk. Kedsell knew that meant, *Challenge me and I'll bust your skull like a china bowl.* He wondered why Donovan was drowning his nerves in the Leghorn instead of hunting down Sunday's new lover, which would be more in his character. Maybe he was afraid of what he'd do if he found him.

"I'll tell you something else, she ain't the same girl now that climbed into bed with Alfieri. The shock turned her into a mystic for two years. She's still kind of off-beat."

"I don't know," Kedsell said. "Arnold Palmer's been struck by lightning three times on the golf course, and he isn't a mystic."

Donovan shrugged.

He never did get a better explanation. Or any other. One night, much later, after he and Sunday were finally lovers and he'd moved into her house, she was walking around in her blue bare-back night gown, and he was sitting at the kitchen table, and when she opened the fridge for a Pepsi he asked her how she got the scar.

She turned and let the fridge door swing slowly shut without getting the soda, and she gave him her rarest face, unreadable as ancient scripture. "You telling me you don't know?" Which was almost exactly what Donovan had said.

He sat up straight. "No. I mean, yes, I'm telling you I don't know."

"What do you think?" she said. Then she opened the fridge again, but this time she took out one of her Seagram's Coolers, picked up her cigarettes from the table. And walked out on the back porch to sit in a chair and drink it and smoke. He could see the back of her head through the screen door, and moths circling the light above her, and a frantic June bug banging the screen. He didn't go out to her.

Sometimes, when they lay in bed deep in the night, he found himself reaching for her scar with his fingers, wondering what was true. Wondering, when she talked in her sleep, what language he was hearing, those incomprehensible words that garbled out of her mouth as if she were carrying on a high-juiced conversation with somebody back in long-ago Egypt. Was that more mystical stuff?

But that day at Hilford Park, they swam and frolicked for a long time. Then they heard another vehicle coming up the utility access road. Everyone seemed to know at once that it was trouble, and splashed out into the trees and hid, except Kedsell, just putting one wet leg into his underpants when a pickup truck pulled up with two men in the cab and the State Park logo on the door. What are you doing here, kid, they wanted to know. He didn't like being called kid after four years in the army, two of them overseas in Guam.

"I'm putting my clothes on."

"I can see that," the man at the steering wheel said, a trace of humor creeping into his voice. "Where's all the rest of them?"

"Huh? The rest of who?" He was teetering.

The man pointed to a pile of strewn clothes. "All those people."

"They went home," Kedsell said.

That cracked up the two park men, and Kedsell wanted to strangle them both.

Then the man got serious again. "I want you all out of here as fast as you can get your skinny asses into your clothes. This part of the park isn't open to the public. Hear me?"

At that, the man put the pickup truck into reverse, and backed down the utility road.

Kedsell's friends came out of the woods then, and they called him an idiot. Like, why the fuck didn't you run into the trees with us? Only Johnny Fish stuck up for him, like, what the hell was he supposed to do, he was already getting dressed, and all our clothes were strewn around, right in plain sight. Kedsell looked at the crowd of naked people, drunk and hostile except for Johnny. Donovan's penis was in a kind of half-hardon as if it aroused him to seethe at someone. Sunday turned and walked back to the pond and dove in, and the others followed her except for Johnny. Her scar was redder now, almost cranberry, and he wondered if anger or intoxication or physical activity or plain horniness put fire in that zigzag the way such things could put red in someone's face.

Kedsell stood at the edge of the pond and said, "Look pals. If you don't climb out of there, the next visit is going to be from a sheriff, and somebody's got a pocket full of smoke in that pile of clothes."

"They can't do nothing about it," Dorie said.

And Donovan said, "They can't go through our clothes without a warrant, you paranoid asshole."

By now Kedsell was dressed. The scene had become like one of his dreams where a whole town was mad at him, or like the nightmare he'd had after reading the Shirley Jackson story about the stoning of a woman who drew the short straw. He felt in his pocket for his car keys. He told Johnny Fish he was leaving. "You want to go with me?"

Johnny Fish, who for some reason was never called simply by his first name, said he'd better stick with Dorie. "She gets in trouble too quick. You want me to move Mellow's jeep?"

"Nah," Kedsell said. "I think if I go straight it'll come out somewhere."

The path wound for what seemed like miles, skirting between the border of the park and the Reservation, bullet-riddled posted signs nailed to trees along the way marking private property. He drove past the stony foundations of old farmhouses, abandoned long ago and swallowed up by the woods. Someone had told him once that families that lived up here had died in a smallpox epidemic, that the town people had come and torched the houses rather than risk handling the bodies. The sick were suddenly strangers. The thought of it gave him the creeps, even if it did happen several lifetimes ago. Finally the path came to an end at a gravel road, probably Wortendyke Road. But a wooden gate, painted yellow and padlocked, blocked the exit. With a deep ditch on both sides.

He drove his bumper tight up against the gate. Goosing the gas pedal, he pressed it and made it groan. But it was reinforced with a frame of solid wood posts. If he rammed the gate, he'd smash his grill and bust out his headlights. Maybe he was never going to get out of here, goddamn it. Far off, a tractor growled. An animal that looked like a coyote bounded through the brush and disappeared. He got out and popped his trunk lid, grabbed his tire iron. Jamming the pry end under the bolts of the lock's swivel eye hasp, he yanked and leaned his weight on it until he snapped the lock away from the wood post. He pushed the gate and it swung open, whining on its hinges like a kicked dog.

Behind the wheel again, he lit a cigarette first, then turned out onto the gravel road. He drove with his windows down. The weather was dry and he left an enormous wake of dust. At home he could lay out in the back yard with a pitcher of gin and tonic, and smoke a joint. Let the sun burn him all it wanted. He was in town and almost home when he saw Sunday's purse on the seat next to the passenger door, a little bronze-colored zip bag. What the hell? How did that end up there? She hadn't even ridden in his car. Then he remembered he'd seen her sitting in his car smoking hash with Dorie.

He turned around at a gas station, and started back. Then he slowed and pulled over. Damn it, it was her purse, let her come and get it. But no, he wasn't so freewheeling that he could let something like this slide. His nature was always unsettled, his default setting was *anxious,* a bare electric wire in his hands. He knew cops would come and she wouldn't have any ID except the lightning scar and some freckles.

Back on Wortendyke Road, he raised another long cloud of dust. He slowed for the broken gate, and just as he was about to turn he saw the taillights of two sheriff cars driving into the woods on the access path. He watched them until they disappeared. He sat in the gravel road with his directional on, reached over and opened the purse. Inside was a sour smelling, half a liverwurst sandwich. Her hash pipe. About five bucks in change and dollar bills. Eyeliner. A ring of keys. A tiny partial ball of hash in a wad of tin foil. Her birth control pills. Pieces of a broken mirror in one shard of which he saw his own bloodshot eye. And a letter from the electric company: a notice of discontinuation of service for non-payment, and a stamp across it: PAID, with the date of the day before, and a receipt stapled to it that read 4:50 PM; she'd coughed up the cash on the last possible day, at ten minutes to closing. He stuffed everything back in the purse and zipped it.

Now a squid-ink of nausea trickled through his stomach, and he didn't know if it was a result of the rotten sandwich smell, or all the beer. Or just the fact that he had invaded Sunday's intimate space in such a creepy way. On the other hand, by dragging his feet on the way back he'd probably saved her from getting busted for the pipe and the chip of hash.

Later, he heard that the two sheriff cars stopped at the pond. The deputies stood and watched them put their clothes on and then wrote each of them a misdemeanor trespassing ticket. They all got hundred dollar fines. He felt sorry for Johnny Fish, who had stuck around only for Dorie. She actually came close to getting locked up, hollering at the deputies, *You can't give a ticket to an Indian for trespassing. It's our fucking land.*

So that was all Kedsell knew about his wife's scar. He'd read a news story once about three woman at a church picnic who got blasted when lightning hit the tree they were sitting under. Why did they die while Sunday survived a direct strike? If in fact she did get struck. It was part of the storehouse of information that Sunday kept from him. But, for some reason, he was the only one she'd never told. Forget it, Kedsell, she'd said, the next and last time he brought it up. That was another thing, she always called him by his last name.

And now, sipping the wedding champagne, he looked at her and wondered, if he didn't know the answers to such heavy personal issues, were they really even married? Legally, of course. But psychically? Even spiritually?

She said, "Well, you've got the rest of the day off, don't you? Why don't you drive me to work, and pick me up after I close? Like a good husband." She picked the cork from the butter dish and tried to pound it into the bottle with the heel of her hand. But it refused to go in. "Then we can finish this if you want."

He got another old cork out of a kitchen drawer and punched it into the bottle neck. "Will you get back into your wedding dress then?"

She looked confused for a moment, then she laughed. She stood and picked up her purse. "I'll do anything you want, Kedsell." But he knew that was provisional.

He was always holding that bare wire, like most Americans, probably. Sunday, on the other hand, was never scared. Pissed off a lot of the time. But afraid, no. Was that what happened to somebody who survived a lightning strike? As they walked to his car he thought, maybe he'd keep his old tape recorder under the bed, and the next time he heard her talking in that weird language, he'd hit the record button, and try to decipher it later by playing it backward.

Opening the car door, she said, "What are you laughing at, Kedsell?"

"Everything, I guess," he said.

On the
Mountain Road

A man is driving up a mountain road. It's steep, wooded, and here and there it makes abrupt turns. Half a mile from the summit he sees people standing beside the road, steam from under the hood of a car billowing high in the frigid air. The man—his name is Gautieri—stops to help. They are all young men and women, standing around their car. A dog in the back seat is barking viciously, showing his teeth and gums. The dog scares Gautieri, but he tries to ignore it. He lifts the hood while the young people, who are frighteningly gaunt, stand around watching him. Two of them have painted their faces bronze, as if they are from the chorus of a Greek tragedy.

One of the young men (or boys, really, since they look like they ought to be in school) says, "Looks serious, don't it?"

The tallest of the boys has a black eye, and a young woman has a lower lip that is swollen and broken open like a ripe plum. Gautieri notices that they all seem to have putridly bad breath.

"Here's your problem," Gautieri says, pointing to a broken water hose. For some reason the people greet this information with smirks and guffaws.

"Well," says the boy with the black eye, "I guess we gotta switch cars now, don't we?"

And with that, they all rush and get into Gautiri's car, the girls grabbing their purses out of their dying vehicle and the boys hitching up their pants. The boy with the black eye claims the driver seat. Gautiri hollers and tries to open one door and another, but the young people have locked all the doors of his car and are grinning at him through the glass. He jumps in front of the car, but then leaps away again when the driver lurches the car ahead. It all happens in about twenty seconds, and Gautieri realizes the boy would have run him down. The thieves drive away up the mountain. And probably down the other side to town. They'll probably drive to town and wreck his car.

The steam is losing its vehemence, but rivulets of green coolant running from the broken car run down the mountain road as if the car's life is trickling away. Like its eyes should be closing in death.

The dog, who looks like an awful mix of beagle, collie, and gargoyle, is still barking inside the broken-down car, showing his teeth. Gautiri curses the dog. And it is at that moment he remembers he has a gun. All this time he's had a Colt pistol in a shoulder harness under his coat. In fact, when he pulled over to help the young people, he had been on his way to a firing range in a wooded clearing at the mountain top. He meets his friends up there on Saturday mornings, and they target practice on a straw-stuffed gorilla and bear. Then they usually drive down the mountain to town to eat lunch and drink scotch. His friend Rodney drinks martinis. But the rest of them drink scotch.

He pulls the gun out now and looks at it. He could have shoved it under those punks' noses. He could have made them get out of the car and lie face down in the rivulets of hot Prestone. When they hollered, he'd have told them to shut up. And if they didn't, he'd have fired a bullet into the asphalt between somebody's legs and made him shit his pants. He could have made them all strip, made them all screw in the road. But he shakes his head, amazed that he would even think of doing such things.

Although it's freezing cold, his face is covered with sweat. He reaches in his pocket for his cell phone, and realizes he'd left it in his stolen car.

The dog is barking so furiously now that he's salivating all over a side window. Gautieri opens the rear door, and the dog immediately rears back.

He says, "Come on, get out."

Slowly, the dog inches forward and then slithers out on

the road, looking up at him and snarling.

"All right, all right," he says.

As the animal backs away, still showing its teeth, he removes the gun from his holster and levels it at the dog.

Now what am I going to do with you?

"You're not my problem, you understand? Go on, get out of here."

He looks in the car to see if they left a cell phone. But there is nothing but magazines and soda cans.

He holsters his gun and begins walking up the mountain. His friends must be already at the range, since he himself was running late before he got into this ridiculous mess. When he gets there he'll tell them the problem and borrow one of their phones and call the police. His friends will tell him he was stupid for getting mixed up with a bunch of creeps, as if they wouldn't stop to help a broken down motorist.

The dog is snapping behind him, right at his heels. He turns, "What the hell is the matter with you? Go on." He kicks at it, but that only seems to make it come after him harder. He tries throwing stones at it. He yells at it louder. When it gets his trouser leg in its teeth, he pulls the gun again. There is a moment, in which they look at each other.

The explosion kicks hard and it sounds about ten times louder than at the firing range, and echoes off the mountain. He draws his lungs full of air. He's never shot anything before, other than a target. Not even a squirrel. Now this pile of fur at his feet. For the first time he sees that the dog has a collar, red with little steel spikes. Bending, he tugs at it, turning it—careful to avoid the blood from where the bullet drilled through the top of the dog's head—until he finds the buckle. And still holding the gun in his right hand, he unbuckles the collar with his left, and holds it up, the tags for its rabies and distemper shots dangling like Milagros. Cagney, his name is, according to the tags.

"Cagney," he says. "Interesting name."

The collar hangs like a rattlesnake hide. Holstering his gun, he puts the collar around his own neck, and snugs it and buckles it. It is the oddest sensation he has felt in years. A dog collar around his neck. He imagines himself standing in front of his wife. What the hell is *that*, she'll say. And he'll say, *Cagney's collar*. Oh, and his friends up at the firing range? *What the fuck*, Gautieri, they'll say. And he'll say, *That's right, what the fuck. That's exactly right.*

"What the fuck," he says now to the pile of fur.

It's another mile to the shooting range. He decides to stay put until another car comes.

In about a half hour he hears a car coming down the road. He's about to take the collar off. They'll stop, probably, and ask him if he's broken down, and there he'll

be, a middle-aged man with a dog collar on. He could get down on all fours and say, *My name is Cagney. This car is broken and my owners have fled. Can you give me a lift to town?*

The car does stop, in the middle of the road. It is his own car and all the kids are piling out of it. The boy with the black eye tosses something to him. Gautieri catches it and sees that it is his cell phone. They're all laughing. And as they climb out of the car they are pushing one another, and carrying food bags from McDonalds.

"Thanks for the car," the boy says. "We used your phone to call a tow truck."

Then the boy sees the pile of fur. One by one the others see it and stop.

THE ZEN ADVENTURE
OF GERALD RILEY

My friend, Gerald Riley, went over the wall, as they say in Zen circles. What that means is, he escaped from a *sesshin*—a silent meditation retreat. At about one in the morning he opened a window next to his bunk in the monastery Guest House and squeezed out, dropping eight feet to the grass, and rolled. From there he climbed over a brick wall, kicking and grabbing until he fell on the other side by the sidewalk. Believe me, this was an almost superhuman feat for him. Gerald is fifty-eight and looks it. His waistline has exceeded his inseam for so many years he doesn't even think about dieting anymore. He started walking down the sidewalk, keeping an eye out for a taxi.

Poor Gerald, I thought, when I heard about it. I'd gone to a *sesshin* the year before, and I know how tough they are. You're locked in a monastery for seven days and nights, sitting motionless on a little *zafu* cushion, staring at a blank wall and keeping your mouth shut. They get you up at four in the morning to do that. Once in a while a little man with a shiny bald head comes along and spanks you sharply on the back with a stick called a *kyōsaku* to make sure you're not getting too comfortable. There may be fifty other people in there with you, but the silence makes you feel like you're hiking alone to the North Pole.

Most people get through *sesshins* all right, and even come away with a little pearl of peace in their hearts, which I guess is the least you should expect from such an ordeal. But others don't hack it.

I didn't think a *sesshin* was a good idea for Gerald. I'm not talking about his weight. A lot of fat people go to *sesshins* and do just fine; some reach enlightenment just like a skinny person. But Gerald likes his creature comforts, his fresh-ground coffee and newspaper in the morning, some leisure time on the john, and lunch at the Squirrel Hole where he favors a Dubonnet with a steak sandwich. Still, he was determined to go. You see, his ex-wife Elicia— Argentinean, and gorgeous—had moved from Pittsburgh to Georgia just to be near the Savannah River Zen Monastery and join their *sesshins* whenever they held them for people outside the monastic order—men and women—seven times a year. She was making herself over from the inside out. Their marriage had ended some months before, possibly because Gerald couldn't imagine giving over the dark and dualistic world of business for chanting the sutras. But he missed her dreadfully, and it choked him up when he heard she was even thinking of becoming a Zen nun. He bought a plane ticket to Atlanta and caught the AAA shuttle to Augusta.

I called him before he left. I said, "Gerry, does Elicia know you're coming?"

He answered, "It's not up to me to tell her I've decided to work on my soul."

But it turned out to be tougher than he'd imagined. The *sesshin* he signed up for started on a Saturday night, and by the next night his knees and hips were on fire from the medieval sitting posture they forced on him; he was trembling from caffeine and alcohol withdrawals, and tormenting himself by mentally undressing Elicia who sat four cushions away deep in meditation. Was she shocked to see him there? He couldn't tell because she didn't so much as twitch her eyelid when they passed in a hallway on their way to and from visits with the teacher, Isan-Roshi. Elicia carried the rule against speaking to the far bounds of the figurative.

He'd followed her bliss into hell.

"What did you expect?" I asked him later.

But he just shook his head.

The taxi he flagged carried him straight to Augusta's notorious Broad Street, where there is a steamy strip joint about every twenty feet. He went into The Basket of Dollies where he settled his girth into a chair at a huge table on which a sleek young woman—Debrina was her name—danced wildly and feathered off what flimsy clothes she wore to start. Seeing the fat man with his elbows on the table, she bent over in front of him, shaking her shaved crotch near his nose while simultaneously taunting him with her face between her knees—hissing, running her tongue and gnashing her teeth. She was so close he could hear—even under the hammering rock music—her two cheap metal crosses on a chain around her neck, dinging faintly as they struck together. Gerald's glasses steamed. Trembling, he tucked a fifty-dollar bill under her garter, where it stuck to her sweaty thigh along with all the one-dollar notes the poorer young boys had stuck there. When she saw it, she smiled and kissed his forehead and mussed his hair. Gerald's heart pounded dangerously.

He'd never been to a strip joint before—completely out of his character. Or, so he told me; and I believed him. Going there was his reaction to being locked in the monastery, the enforced silence, and the pain of seeing the dead-silent Elicia. Other than in movies and magazines, he'd never seen a naked woman before, except Elicia. And even with her—dear God!—he'd never stared eyeball to pussy, which he'd known only by touch.

Getting back into the monastery was another hurdle.

After the taxi dropped him off, he scaled the wall again, bashing his shins. Then, realizing that the Guest House window was an impossible reach, he walked into the shadowy inner yard where he crawled under a spruce tree and sat, resting his back against its trunk. Exhausted, he dozed, got up once or twice to piss in the Japanese flowers, and slipped back under the tree to sleep. He dreamed himself back in the taxi, pulling up in front of the monastery; but, being too weary to pull the door handle, he rode helplessly away again.

He nodded awake at 4 a.m. when he saw the senior monk coming down the path from the Main House in his bare feet and robe, with his big iron bell that sounded like a cowbell. Crouching low, Gerald watched the monk enter the Guest House— as was his regular morning ritual—to jangle the bell outside the door of the women's bunk room, then stalk directly through the men's room ringing it next to the beds, jarring men upright.

As they stumbled outside like bugs after fumigation, the monk ordered them into a silent circumambulation around the inner yard, a brisk stride in the chilly morning air to get their blood moving. When the monk was looking in another direction, Gerald left his black shoes and socks under the tree, and stepped out of the shadows to join the line. His bare feet chafed on the cinder path, and several times he bit down on a curse before it blurted from his lips. Almost diametrically opposite him in the circle was Elicia, thin as a small tree in her robe, hands folded softly against her *rakusu*—a kind of apron over her breast that signified her commitment to the Dharma. She'd begun braiding her dark brown hair in a long rope, which made her seem even taller and thinner, yet somehow stronger.

She used to call him Sugarbelly, though that part of their past seemed impossible now. One of the last things she'd ever allowed him do for her was wash her feet, plagued with plantar warts, not so long ago. He'd massaged her arches and tendons—hard as little cables—and put medicated pads on the warts. She'd flinched then. Later she'd insisted on washing them herself. Now he wondered how her feet were holding up. Maybe they were as galling as his own; or maybe in her blissful state she didn't mind her pain as she used to.

The day was brutal. He nodded off on his cushion, taking blow after blow on his back from the monitor with that damned *kyōsaku* until he felt a horrible urge to grab it away and use it to beat the man's head bloody. Later in the morning he slumbered during Isan-Roshi's homily, though he heard parts he found dumbfounding: about a young Buddhist—centuries ago—who stood barefoot in snow and ice all night outside a monastery before he was finally accepted in as a student. The very thought of it made his feet numb with cold. Why did it all have to be so damned hard? By evening, when the *dokusan* bell rang and he trudged down the dark hallway to get into line to see Isan-Roshi, he felt better, like he'd accumulated enough nods over the day to be almost rested. As if the booze the night before had even done him good.

The line moved sadistically slow, and when his turn finally came he entered the *dokusan* room where Isan-Roshi sat on his cushion under the grimacing portrait of an old Japanese Zen master. Or *probably* Japanese. Gerald told me later that, after a while, everyone at the monastery looked Japanese to him, like the Roshi himself. Maybe it was just the shaved heads, he mused; or the robes and the erect postures; or maybe their features were really changing from eating the pickled vegetables and rice. Or, just his imagination. All mirrors were covered up or put away during *sesshin*, so he couldn't check to see if he was starting to look as Japanese as everyone else.

Everyone, that is, except Elicia.

Gerald bowed to the teacher, then did a roly-poly prostration on the floor before settling himself on the cushion in front of Isan.

"Hah, Gerald-san," Isan said, "you know what you doing here?"

That question hit Gerald right in the eye-between-his-eyes. This was his sixth or seventh interview with Isan already, but up to now Gerald had asked all the questions. "What am I doing here?" he repeated the question now. "What do you mean, Roshi? I'm sitting in *zazen*, eating flavorless food, and I've been assigned to scrub the first floor toilets."

Isan-Roshi's smile was so broad he thought the bottom of the man's head might fall off. "Good, Gerald-san. Good, good." And he picked up his hand bell and rang it in the air, signally the end of their meeting.

Gerald bowed his way backward out of the room. Somehow he didn't feel that his true self had made any strides in that meeting. If anything, his true self felt more irascible.

That night he couldn't sleep again. Three or four of the other men in the room were snoring like wood chippers. And all he could think of was Elicia: her vagina, her legs, and belly—and her vagina. What if her pussy had been shaved, would it have looked like that little tart Debrina's in The Basket of Dollies? While the others snored and bubbled, he reached for his clothes on the chair next to his bed, pulled them under the covers and wiggled into them. Lastly, he reached for his shoes, and threw them out the window.

But this time he walked for blocks and saw no taxi. Only a few cars passed at all. A black man approached on the sidewalk carrying a paper bag in his arms. Gerald stopped him and asked if he had a car.

The man hesitated, and said, "A car? No, I ain't got no car."

"None at all? None you can use?"

The man stepped under the streetlight where Gerald could see that he was elderly. He'd thought the man was younger because his step was springy.

"My son's got a car."

"Listen, I'll pay you a lot of money if you'll drive me downtown."

The man squinted. "Mister, are you in some kinda trouble?"

"I don't know. I may be."

At that moment a large black sedan squealed around the corner and sped toward them. Gerald heard the brakes sing, and as the car pulled to a stop next to them, the side window was already descending. "Gerald-san, get in," said a voice.

Gerald froze to the spot. The man walked quickly away. The door of the car opened and Isan-Roshi stepped out and held the front passenger door open for him. He was dressed in plain dungarees and an open L. L. Bean jacket;

and for the first time Gerald realized how small his teacher was—his head came barely to the roof of the car. "Please," he said a little imploringly.

So, Gerald slid into the front seat. Isan-Roshi got into the back. One of the Roshi's senior students was driving, Harmon Smythe, an Englishman with a shaved head who had been the one who opened the monastery's big front door when Gerald arrived the previous Saturday. Gerald had suspected then that he'd smelled the scotch on his breath (Gerald had asked the shuttle driver to drop him off a couple blocks from the monastery where he went into a bar and downed three double-scotches before the *sesshin*). Now Isan told Harmon to drive back to the monastery.

A robed woman was watching out the front door when they pulled up in front of the Main House. Her name was Vera, a nun. She'd been the second person he'd met there, who had also puckered her nose at his breath, but had assigned his number, 38, which identified his bunk, his *zafu*, and was probably the number they'd write on his body-bag if he had a heart attack. Gerald looked at her indignantly as they came in the door, and she turned away, walking ahead to open the door to Isan's office. Somehow everything she did seemed ritualistic to Gerald, even a simple thing like turning a doorknob, and it annoyed him bitterly.

Gerald took a chair. Harmon and Vera stood against the

wall with their arms folded as if at any moment they might have to defend their teacher against a physical attack.

"Now," Isan said, seating himself at his desk. "What you *doing* here?"

At this moment Isan seemed less like a venerable teacher to Gerald than a petty third-world bureaucrat.

"I'm being held against my will," Gerald snarled. "It's a federal offense, just in case you're not familiar with American law."

"I do not prevent you from leaving. But I ask why."

"All right then, I'll be going," Gerald said getting up. "I'll get my stuff out of the Guest House."

"Wait," Isan said, holding up his hand. "You cannot go there at this hour, you will disturb others."

"But I can't leave without my belongings."

"Why not? You did not take them to Basket of Dollies last night."

The hair stood on Gerald's neck. "How do you know where I went? I didn't see you there."

"I have friend drive taxi. Now you tell me what I do *not* know. Why you here?"

Defeated, Gerald flopped down in the chair again and told Isan-Roshi the whole sad business—about Elicia, how he'd lost her and had tried to follow her into her new world, but found it inhospitable. Now he was sorry, and felt like a fool. He wept. "But," he added, glancing quickly from Isan to his two helpers and back again, "I really don't want to leave. I don't want to go home now." He still felt a horrible need for Elicia. But also, he was several days into this damned *sesshin;* and, brutally hard though it was, when he imagined flying home early he saw himself deflated and confused. "I have never been a quitter," he asserted, stiffening himself. Harmon looked bored, like he'd heard this too many times.

"I afraid you must leave," Isan said. "You here for all wrong reasons, Gerald-san."

That was when Gerald, my old friend, threw one of his notorious fits. One of his meltdowns. He doesn't do it often, maybe once every couple years. Elicia must have witnessed more than one. Maybe his fits even contributed to their divorce in a small way. But I've only seen one full-blown performance (at a team-building seminar for the investment firm where we both worked) such as he gave them now. He slammed both fists on Isan's desk, screaming and threatening self-mutilation and suicide; he rolled on the floor beating his head and chest until Harmon and Vera picked him up by the arms and set him collapsed and sobbing back in his chair. Harmon went out and returned with tea on a little tray and gave him a cup. Slowly he regained himself. He sipped—or slurped, rather.

When he finally spoke again, it was like the efforts of a man who had just climbed an exceedingly high ladder, his lungs gasping with something important to say.

"I am prepared," he said, gasping more, "to write a very sizable check to this monastery...to allow me to stay in this *sesshin* until the end." He choked and took a sip and another deep breath before saying, "But on one condition," as if their acceptance was a foregone conclusion. He waited for someone to ask what that condition was. When no one did, he continued, "I must sleep in a private room."

Isan refused the money, but imposed his own conditions. Gerald was moved to an oak-paneled room in the Main House with a four-posted bed. But, beginning the next morning, he was to scrub all the toilets in all the buildings both upstairs and down—a back-breaking task, more Sisyphean than Herculean since, by the time he'd cleaned the last toilet, scrubbing it inside and out, the first was filthy again. To complete it took far more than the regular after-breakfast work hour that was part of the daily routine in *sesshin*, but also the free hour in the afternoon when most Zennies caught a wink of sleep. Even after the last formal sitting ended at 10 pm, when other Zennies wandered off to bed or to dark corners to continue their meditation into the wee hours, Gerald could be seen running between the Main and Guest Houses with his bucket, brushes and rags. He was beyond weary, on another plane altogether in which his last glimmering electrolytes were being depleted. But Gerald was taken now with an almost creepy contentment, focused in a way he hadn't been for years—unless he counted the few minutes he'd spent watching Debrina in The Basket of Dollies. At midnight he collapsed in the oak room bed until the clanging four-o'clock monk came to his door.

"Let me tell you," he told me later, "that little runt Isan knew what the hell he was doing, sticking me on that toilet detail."

Because, although the long hours of sitting on the hard little *zafu* remained torturous—with the silent and self-absorbed Elicia nearby—he now entered long stretches of exhausted meditation in which he was conscious only of his breath, tiding in and out of his shallow lungs. He was awed by the sound and feel of his breath, its thin veil between his mind and soul. And when he cleaned a toilet, he polished it like a pearl. Work and meditation were becoming integrated, and he wondered what effect it would have on his job as a stock analyst when he returned home. (A new power of focus—it would have to help, huh?) When the *dokusan* bell rang the next afternoon, Gerald actually ran down the hallway to get in line to see his teacher, anxious to talk about something that had disturbed his exhausted sleep the night before.

In the yellowish light of the *dokusan* room he fell forward to get the prostration done with, and then clambered onto the cushion. Odors of cleaning and disinfecting solutions wafted up from under his robe.

"Careless," Isan-Roshi said.

"Huh?"

"Sloppy prostration, Gerald-san."

Gerald apologized and offered to do it again, but the Roshi shook his head impatiently.

"Roshi, let me level with you," Gerald began, closing his eyes for a moment, wrinkling his forehead. "Something very strange happened in my sleep. In my dream, I mean. That is, I think I was sleeping. I dreamed that Debrina, the young woman I saw dancing in The Basket of Dollies, came into my room and made love to me. It was so real that I worry it might have actually happened. She might be following me."

Isan-Roshi seemed to ponder this for a moment, twisting his lips in thought. "Is *makyo*," he finally said.

"What? What is *makyo*?"

"Happens in early stage of Zen practice. Illusion. Your mind begin spring cleaning. Carry out garbage. You see crazy things go by."

"I admit I was delirious, Roshi. But I could even hear

her two little crosses ringing together."

What crosses? the Roshi wanted to know. And Gerald explained about the crosses on Debrina's necklaces, such as a religious girl would wear.

"Is *makyo*," he assured Gerald again. "Better be *makyo*, Gerald-san." And he chuckled.

But later, when Gerald slipped back to his room in the Main House to get an extra shirt—it was a chilly evening— he noticed one of the staff working on the front door, apparently changing the lock.

That night, after he cleaned the twenty toilets, or thirty or forty toilets—he lost count—also unplugging some that were choked with combs and sanitary napkins and purloined food hastily disposed of—he collapsed in his bed, immobilized with fatigue. And then, he had the same delirious *makyo*, in which Debrina came into his room in the dark, in a blanket which she dropped at his bedside, and pulling away his covers, took her pleasure on him, her crosses dinging, running that crazed tongue over his face, making him explode inside of her.

Makyo! Makyo! Zen was a screwy world in which both ecstasy and abject pain were disavowed as inconsequential. It thrived on contradictions. They taught him a complicated chant, and then told him to forget it. They strove for awakening by depriving themselves of sleep. Isan sent him to open windows in a room where no windows existed. They talked in riddles of one hand clapping, and, *Does a dog have Buddha nature?* which he seemed to understand only when he was ready to collapse.

He was wakened by the moon, by its round and nearly full orb which had moved into an upper pane of the window near his bed. It had been a long time since he'd looked at the moon, or even noticed it, while living in the city in a galaxy of artificial light. It astonished him now, and made him emotional. For a moment he wondered if Elicia was looking at it too, then he decided he didn't care. *He* was looking at it now—that was all that mattered. Although it was a little fuzzy. He felt around on the nightstand for his glasses but couldn't find them. Maybe it wasn't important if it was fuzzy. In a homily, Isan-Roshi had quoted an old Zen admonishment: Don't confuse the moon with the finger that points at it. So, he would not confuse it with his glasses either.

Then came the bell. He could hear it jangling at the Guest House. Jangle-clang. The monk would be back here any minute shaking it at his own door. He decided that for once he would beat that crazy monk to the draw—he would get up *now*. But when he rolled toward the other side of his bed, he ran into something solid in his sheets, heavy. It grunted and stirred; and then it also heard the bell, and said, "Oh!" and jolted upright in the bed. "Oh!" she cried again. "Oh my God!" Gerald was on his hands and knees now, peering in the dark. This was no *makyo*, he was certain of that. Two little bells dinged together as his visitor searched frantically around the room in the dark for her clothes.

He called out to her to wait. That it was okay. He didn't mind.

"I don't care what you think, you dolt," came a lovely, heart-squeezing, Argentinian accent. At last she found her robe in the dark, and pulled it on over her head. "I'll come back for my other clothes later. Okay? Do you hear me?"

He said, "Yes, Elicia."

She bolted for the door, calling back, "Why did you have to follow me down here?"

As she threw open the door, he saw her stop short in the glaring hallway light. He could barely see the monk, but he could hear the bell's clatter go silent as if in shock.

They sat more or less together in chairs facing Isan-Roshi's desk. The venerable teacher hadn't arrived yet, but Harmon served them tea, which seemed like an act of sympathy while also giving the occasion an air of Zen officialdom, even while they waited. But Gerald refused the tea. He was even more indignant than he was two nights before when he'd accused Isan of holding him captive. This was undignified, like being dragged to the principal's office; and he was ready to take off Isan's head. But then he saw how distressed Elicia was, how her fingers trembled when she sipped her tea, and he felt tenderly sorry. Yes, he really had imposed himself on her world. He'd made a terrible mistake and ruined things for her. He told her he was sorry.

"Oh," she said dismissively, "there's nothing to apologize for."

"But you seem so disconsolate."

She struggled to take another sip. "That is because I am disconsolate."

"That is why I am sorry."

"Well, then, it's up to you if you want to feel that way, but there's no need."

When Isan came in, his face was flushed with annoyance. After all, they had broken one of the primary rules of *sesshin* at Savannah River Zen Monastery. For the duration of the *sesshin* you are to remain celibate.

"You both have wasted time," Isan began. "Terrible waste!" Then he strode out of the room again.

Though it was barely sun-up, their belongings were brought to the front door of the Main House where

Gerald sat lacing up his shoes, and Elicia looked silently out a window at the street. The taxi arrived just as daylight outlined the magnolia tree in the yard of a nearby house. When the main door swung shut behind them, he heard its new lock snap hard, automatically.

They slid into the back seat, and the cabby asked, Where to? Gerald started to say the bus terminal (Elicia lived in Madison, maybe an hour away, and the same bus would go on to Atlanta). But she interjected, "I'm so hungry." So Gerald said to take them downtown.

"I've been starving all week," she added. "I just couldn't get enough food. I cannot believe it, but I even stole some out of the kitchen. I was nearly caught with it, so I flushed it down the toilet."

Gerald was relieved to see it wasn't the same cabby who had taken him to the strip joint earlier in the week, nor the one who brought him back—one of whom had tattled. He would have been tempted to whack him all over the head and back, like certain old Zen Masters were known to do to bad little students.

They arrived at a cafe just as it was opening, where they ordered a breakfast of eggs and grits, to which Gerald added sausage gravy. He ate hungrily and loudly, guzzling coffee, and watched Elicia pick at the food she'd declared herself so famished for. He thought they needed conversation, so he talked about the house and the new curtains he'd bought since she'd moved out. Actually, the place was a mess, like a movie set for a story of a man struggling with loneliness— half-bags of cookies everywhere, garbage overflowing. His shirts and slacks were clean only because he took them to the dry cleaners, while he bought new socks and undershorts for each day, throwing the dirty veterans into a spare bedroom where a pyramid of linen grew. So he told her only about the new curtains, and a new power-chair that hummed and gave him massages.

Elicia set her fork on the table. "That is so manipulative, Gerald."

"What is?" he asked, shocked.

"To tell me about the house at a time like this."

He was stunned. But then he understood: she was right. This wasn't supposed to be happening to them— this eating together, sitting together at a table or doing anything else together, ever again. At the bottom of all their old bickering, somewhere in the tangle of their struggles to explain themselves to each other, was a reason for their failure, sure as there's a worm in the bottom of a tequila bottle. It's there, why explain it?

"What are you going to do?" he asked.

"Do?" she looked up, as if the verb were the name of a stranger thrown in her face.

"Yes. What will you do when you get home? I mean, how are you going to deal with all of this?"

She shook her head. "I don't know. I just feel so humiliated."

Outside they were surprised to see the taxi still at the curb where they'd left it. The cabby said he'd had nothing else to do but wait. Now he drove them on to the bus terminal. And as they rode, Gerald noticed the moon still hanging in the brightening sky, faint now, almost like a face in a double-exposed photo. The moon that he'd been so startled and happy to see was waning again. "Goodbye, moon," he said aloud, not caring what Elicia would think.

At the terminal he got out and helped Elicia with her bag, and he said his farewell.

"You're not taking the bus?" she asked, startled.

He shook his head, and he was surprised to see her look of disappointment. No, he told himself firmly, watching her walk to the door of the terminal and disappear inside, I am not getting on that bus. Then he got back in the cab. He sat for a minute, thinking and stroking his chin. Finally, he said, "Take me where I can buy some ice, will you?"

The cab pulled into a gas station, where Gerald bounded inside and came out minutes later with four enormous bags of crushed ice in his arms. When the puzzled cabby got out and picked up one bag that Gerald dropped, he was promised a big tip. "Back to the monastery. Please."

They lugged the bags to the front door of the Main House. Gerald could only hope the four bags would be enough. One by one, he broke them by slamming them against the iron railing, letting the crushed ice spill out on the front stone steps like a little borrowed winter.

"I thought you were going to throw a big party with this ice," the cabby mumbled.

"No party today."

The cabby shrugged.

"You mind getting rid of these for me?" Gerald asked, handing the broken bags to the cabby. Then he thanked the man, and gave him all the cash he had in his wallet. The man looked confused, but he shrugged again. Gerald waited until the taxi had driven out of sight before he took off his shoes and socks.

Later, Gerald would describe for me the startled look on the face of the monk who opened the door to answer his pounding—to see my old friend standing in the crushed ice, in his bare feet, begging to be admitted.

COME BACK, LITTLE HOG

He was a hard worker. That was the main thing he had going for him. Not skill with numbers or words. He lied about finishing high school, and lied about his age to get a Social Security Number and a job. The way boys once lied in order to join the French Foreign Legion, or the Royal Romanian Mounted Guard, because anything was better than life at home. He was hired onto the night shift in a foundry that held big defense contracts. They made iron shells for fragment-bombs. He had to spell his first name, Japha, twice for the woman who typed up his first time card, a name his mother snatched from a map of the Holy Land in her Bible. The job was like working in hell: hot, dirty, the air stank of sulfur and burnt metals, a constant ear-splitting *bonkaa-bonkaa-bonkaa* raged in his head, and men's faces were blistery red from the intense fires. Each night for eight hours there was no relief. Even the drinking fountain gushed hot water. And the foremen walked around laughing at the sweating men.

There a night janitor told him a story he never forgot.

It was about a horseplay incident that had occurred years before on the same shift. One night, the janitor claimed, some men had wrestled a hapless guy to the floor, yanked down his pants and fired an air hose up his ass. It had blown his intestines out like a tire, and he'd bled to death on the concrete. The moral of the story was, Japha guessed, don't screw around on the job. Being a kid, he swallowed the story in a gulp.

But he was also a drifter, and over the next couple years he heard the same tale at several other jobs, a bottling plant, a peanut butter warehouse, a gasket factory, an elevator factory, and one or two other places. In some versions, the victim was a family man with six kids, all of whom ended up on the street after Daddy's guts were blown out. In others he was a retarded boy with a broom. And in one he was a young man who'd been born with a dog's head. In more detailed versions, the men paused to put a little axel grease on the nozzle before they rammed it home. Finally, he understood that it wasn't a warning against horseplay at all. It was a message that he was a marked man. That his short little legs and pink skin, both due to a birth defect, and sparse bristly hair, all which inspired men to call him Hog, also made them want to hold him down and shove an air hose up his ass. Turn him into a pink balloon and go pop in the air. The rest of the implied message was, would you please get the fuck out of here before we get to the point where we can't control ourselves?

He kept moving, but everywhere he went they had a compressor rumbling in a corner and a long air hose, and he always landed on the dangerous night shift, and everywhere he heard the same story. Plus, wherever he went he was called Hog as if everyone already knew him. Sometimes men left cans of axel grease open near his workstation, and when they walked by they'd grin at him.

Hog had a job in a dog food factory in the outskirts of a farm town, as the Nightshift Mule, Labor Grade 14C and a member of the Aerospace, Poultry Packing, and Dock Workers Union Amalgamated, AFL-CIO, which meant he used finger-burning solvent and rags to clean the meat chewing machines that turned beef gristle and chicken organs and pork lung and horse brains into a pate for canned dog food. After cleaning, he oiled the joints and pushed the reset button that started the machines chewing meat again, *hunk-a hunk-a hunk-a*. If the chewing was smooth and rhythmic he went on to the next set of jaws.

He lived in an abandoned car in a junk lot beside an out-of-business gas station at a cross street near the center of the tiny town. Boys regularly tried to break into the car and molest the pink man in his sleep, and so he acquired his first gun, a .22 caliber pistol which he kept under the floor mat beneath candy wrappers and hamburger bags and soda cans, and he waved it in their noses when they came and woke him up in the middle of the day.

One daybreak in September he punched out and walked back to sleep in the car, but when he reached the gas station it was open, back in business again. It had happened all at once. Lights were on. Cars were stopping and getting gas, the garage door was open and a man was in the bay using an air hose to inflate a couple tires. He turned and smiled at Hog standing in the open door. "What can I do for ya?" he asked. But Hog backed away, and ran to the woods where he lay all day on soft pine needles, yet tossing and turning, not dozing for more than a half hour at a time.

Hog bided his time until night when he could slip back to the car, get his gun and extra clothes and hide them outside the plant until he could find another place to sleep. But the station was still open a little before 11 p.m. when he walked by on his way to the dog food factory. People swarming, cars filling with gas, men talking and drinking Cokes and eating candy bars from the machines and bragging. Two girls, a big redheaded one and a skinny blonde held bowling-ball bags in one hand and their purses in the other, like they had just left the alleys and were stopping off at the gas station to listen to the men brag. Girls made Hog uneasy. He especially hated waitresses who looked at him like a plugged toilet. So he kept walking to work. He had to punch the clock by 11.

When the break whistle blew, Hog went and sat in a corner of the lunchroom. He would have stayed in production during break, but whenever he did that the union steward chased him out. It was against union rules not to leave your work area during break.

"Where's your lunch tonight, Hog?" a man asked with his mouth full of sandwich.

Hog shook his head and grunted. He was famished, but he didn't want to admit it.

"How about a little sausage?" a man asked him.

Almost involuntarily, Hog looked up to see the man squeezing himself in the crotch. The room erupted in guffaws, and Hog stalked off to the latrine to sit in a stall with the door closed until the whistle blew.

When he woke, he could hear the *hunk-a hunk-a* machines grinding their teeth on the funky gristle and organ meat. What time was it? Had he missed the whistle? He slipped out of the latrine heading quickly toward production. On his way, he passed the broad window of Wayne Waller's office and saw the night foreman fast asleep in his chair. So, he wasn't going to be in trouble with him; but yet, without Waller slipping around the plant, anything was liable to happen.

"Hey Hog, you have a good dream?" someone bellowed as he walked among the chewing machines.

And someone else sang rock-a-bye piggie in the treetop.

A moment later Hog felt two pairs of arms grab him by his elbows, and he was hustled forward, his short legs taking two or three steps for every single stride of the men who had hold of him. When he stumbled, they held him aloft momentarily like a child dangling between two parents in a hurry. Ahead, he saw a sheet of cardboard on the floor, a man standing with a hose, and another man holding a can of axel grease in his gloves. They were smiling like it was a river baptism. The men's grip was like iron cables, and they pressed him down shrieking on the cardboard and another pair of hands yanked down his trousers. Nickels and quarters rolled out of his pockets.

"This won't hurt much," said the man with the hose, and he jammed the hose into Hog's ass.

Nothing happened.

"Hey, turn the damn compressor on," one of the men yelled.

"It's always on," hollered another. "Round the clock."

"The fork lift's sittin' on the hose. Move it, goddamn it."

The distraction gave Hog a chance to squirm, and though the men's hands instantly pressed down hard, he'd gained an inch of momentum and found himself on his feet, and drove his head into a man's testicles. Pulling up his pants, he ran headlong, shouts following him around the chewing machines. At one point he used a coal shovel to fend off two men. He saw the overhead door to the meat locker standing open, and he bolted through and ran among the racks of pork lungs. Two men followed in close pursuit.

"What's going on here?" came a shout. "What's this door doing open?" It was Waller's voice. "You're letting all the cold out of that room." The men who had chased him in there came skulking out again, making the excuse that they'd heard something in there and they'd gone to check it out, and Waller closed the door, saying, "Yeah, yeah, yeah. One of the pork lungs came to life, huh? What's this cardboard doing on the floor? Somebody's gonna slip on it."

Hog was in the dark now, with the shovel still in his hands, feeling his way along a wall to a door that let him into the shipping and receiving department, which was also dark, to the back dock where trucks arrived in the day with fresh pork lungs, cow's eyes, and pork bellies, horse guts and chicken necks, barrels of carp and cow bones, and took cases of canned dog food away to supermarkets. The loading dock door was padlocked, but with the shovel Hog easily pried open the flimsier receiving clerk's entrance.

He was outside, and running for the center of town.

He knew that within minutes Waller would be looking for him, dumb to the fact that the men were trying to kill him. The night was overcast, but partially starlit, with a three-quarter moon. He reached the four corners and saw with relief the gas station was closed. The small town, which had little more than a store and a feed mill and a few houses, was dark. He opened the car, and found the pistol and clips under the floor mat. The hell with the rest of his clothes. He'd find other clothes somewhere else.

Then he noticed several cars parked close to the gas station, on the shadow side away from the street lights of the intersection. He knew that when gas station people fixed cars they often left them for the night with the keys hidden in some idiotically obvious place so that their owners could pick them up early in the morning. He riffled through a couple, looking under the floor mats, in the ashtray, over the visor, but found nothing but the bills for repair work. Searching was risky, since the overhead light came on in the cars when he opened the doors, and someone would see him sooner or later. An old red Ford station wagon reminded him of a car his father used to drive, was still driving when Hog had left home. But he found no keys in it either. He was about to slam the door when he noticed a lump under the floor mat on the passenger side. Ah-ha!

Now he had cold keys in his hand. He started the

vehicle and backed it out of its space, but it sputtered and stalled after a blip of Elvis' voice wrung from the radio. He restarted it. They didn't fix this one too good. He put it in neutral and goosed the gas until great balls of smoke burst from its ass. With the window down, Elvis blared: *I'm just a hunk-a hunk-a burnin' love.*

He spun the car around in the gas station lot and entered the street where it stalled again, sideways across both lanes. This time when he twisted the key it only growled. Far down the road he saw lights approaching. He jumped out of the car, left the door open and ran in the direction of the factory, the radio still howling, *I'm just a hunk-a hunk-a burnin' love, aaaaaah.* So, he wasn't leaving town as quickly as he'd hoped.

Reentering the plant through the same clerk's door, he found the door leading back into the meat locker and waited until the big overhead door opened—as he knew it did every twenty minutes or so. He watched a man on a forklift drive in, slowly hook his forks to a rack of cold meat. Before the man could back out, Hog slipped around behind him and scurried into production.

The clock above the big meat-chewers read 3:51 a.m., and he crouched behind an I-beam pillar near the lunchroom, breathing fast and deep as a blowfish, until he heard the 4:15 coffee break whistle and heard the men coming down the aisle from production. When they were in range of about ten feet, he stepped out and stood in full view of them, eight men. A puzzled look came over some, others looked indifferent.

"Well, lo and behold," said one.

"Hey, little Hog," another said. "Back for more?"

When Hog pulled his pistol, a mix of gasps and grunts came up the men's throats. They said, Look, Hog. Look, *dude*. They tried backing away, but he kept advancing on them. One tried an explanation. We were only putting you through an initiation. That was all it was. After that, well, what the fuck, Hog. I mean, holy shit, man.

Hog sang, *"I'm just a hunk-a hunk-a burning love, aaaaaaah!"*

"What the hell's going on *now*?" he heard Waller's voice coming up the aisle behind him.

Hog spun around on a snap impulse and fired three shots into the foreman's legs. *Crack-crack-crack.* He had never shot a gun before, and his vision in those moments was distorted like a dream, but he saw bloody holes burst open in Waller's pant legs. Shock and confusion waved across the foreman's face as he crumpled into a sitting posture on the floor like someone had pulled a chair out from under him, and then he rolled onto his side. Hog dashed past the bleeding foreman, past the lunchroom and time clock and foreman's station and main offices and out into the night again. He ran for the woods. Hog had always been told he had a bad heart—more of the stuff of his birth defects. But now a new energy filled his arms and legs, and he realized he was drawing on strength that he hadn't known he had, and he knew he could run all night and all the next day. He burrowed under fences and splashed across creeks. He would run out of this used up life and into a new one in which he would carry a gun. And he was all through working for a living.

To the north the night horizon was reddened by a city that he had never been to. On the highway the sound of sirens rose, their melodies weaving, crying in the trees. Come back Hog, they sang. Little Hog, we won't hurt you.

AIR BAGGAGE

The crew throws the stowed bags onto the flight bridge, and everyone grabs one. Warned as we do by a sign that reads, *Beware: many bags look alike.* As do yours and mine. So you're careful, or think you are. Until you get home and find under the zipper my private interior of clothes, cologne, extra shoes. I have your bag too, and I open and close you, and you close me, quietly startled. So, I know your fragrances, your scent, what you were reading before you packed to go home, the disorder of your lingerie suggesting you stuffed your bag in a hurry, in a fury. Among your silk I find, finally, your red business cards with your name and number.

Now I'm the bodiless voice that phones you. "Hello? Talia Greenman? I have your suitcase. We must have been on the same flight."

You say, "Oh, um, who are you?" You sound grateful, but wary and upset.

While I drive to your house I think about how I won't look like the man you expect me to be. And you won't look like the woman that I imagined when I opened your bag on my bed. But voices and faces rarely match, as any criminologist will tell you. This is just one more indignity of travel. Many times when you've passed through airport security you've had to take off your shoes, open your suitcase for a tough-looking uniformed man, and once a uniformed woman ran her fingers under your breasts. You've stood before the denuding machine with your hands raised as if in surrender. But this is different. Seriously different. Because now it's dark, and I am on my way to your house. Maybe I have a knife or a gun. Or vice-like hands.

You place a quick call to a neighbor woman you know well. "Christine," you say, "look, honey, I just got home from Miami, and my luggage got switched with some guy. You know what I mean? Yeah, that's right, he called and he's on his way over here. Yep, you got it, I'm scared. Hurry over here, okay? All I know about him is, the heels on his cheap shoes are worn down and I like his cologne."

Christine is there in five minutes, laughing hilariously.

"Look," you say, "it might turn out to be funny, and it might not."

She pours herself a drink and parks herself on your couch while you peek through the curtains at a car that pulls up at the curb. You think it'll be just your luck that I'll turn out to be the burly, bearded, eighty-year-old who sat in front of you and exuded odors of booze. In fact, a man who looks very much like him gets out of the car, and stands in the snow by the curb.

"Shit," you say.

Christine says, "I know how you feel, believe me. I've had some real whacks coming up my sidewalk."

But the man does not even look at your house. He crosses the street and in a moment is out of sight.

The red blink-blink of an airplane arcs overhead as I turn onto your street. Then the plane disappears in the cloud cover as heavy snow begins to fall. As I park my car and walk toward your door I leave man-prints in the fresh snow, like my kind have been leaving in snow and sand and mud for hundreds of thousands of years.

Meanwhile Christine has suggested that she pose as you. So you sit on the couch while she opens the door and smiles at me. "Wow. You know, it's really nice of you to bring my luggage back. I really mean it, honey. This is a rare kindness."

I'm a little startled at the sudden shift in demeanor from the wary voice I talked to on the phone. She invites me in and offers me a drink. The three of us sit around the kitchen table. After a couple drinks I get my nerve up. I tell her I have one question. "Did you leave Miami in a big hurry?"

Christine looks at me, puzzled. "Why, honey?"

I cough. "Well, the general disorder in the suitcase, like someone just flung her stuff in there."

That cracks her up. "I sure did, mister. You want to know why? Did you investigate any further. I mean, like, did you sniff my undies, Fido?" Then she laughs so hard that she almost drops her drink. She looks over at you and says, "He's turning beet red."

I'm upset and I protest. I say it never even occurred to me to so such a thing. I deny, deny, deny.

Christine says, "It's okay, honey. I've had weirder guys than you sniffing me. In fact, we were just sniffing your stuff before you showed up."

Now we're all laughing. We call ourselves dogs. Sniff, snort, sniff, snort. I can't believe my own behavior. I mean, here we are down on our hands and knees now sniffing each other.

Then she says, "Hey, what's your pedigree anyway? I don't let just any kind of mutt in here to sniff *me*."

It's not until the next day that I realize the ruse, when you come over to my house to give me my own suitcase, which I forgot to take with me after I woke up in your house on the couch sometime past midnight. But here you are. After I get over my initial surprise at who is really who, you say, "I'm sorry, I never would have done those things to you on my own. I can't undo last night. I mean it was, like—*Christine*, you know what I mean?"

I shrug and say, "I'm sorry about the mess we made."

You say, "It's all right." But we both admit it was a special night, and we talk about it for a few minutes, referring hesitantly to "the stuff we did," because neither of us has a vocabulary for some of the activities.

"Anyway," you say finally, "here's your bag. We'd better be more careful at the airport in the future."

After you leave, I carry the suitcase upstairs to my bedroom. While I'm taking a much-needed shower, I wonder if I'll ever see you again. Now that I'm thinking it through and washing off the sticky residue, I don't know whether I'm glad Christine isn't you or not. In fact, I'm pretty pissed off at having the trick played on me, and I wish I had understood my feelings while you were still here so that I could have told you off. I mean, what the hell is wrong with you? You must have thought I was stupid. You'll probably be cracking jokes about it with Christine for weeks. One of you will say, *Woof-woof*, and the other will say, *Roof-roof*, and then dissolve into hysterics.

Then I pop the suitcase open to put my stuff away. But—it's all your stuff. Your dirty silks, a red blouse, some slacks and a nude bra, your cheap novel, just as I'd seen it all the night before. Your scent is suddenly blossoming all over the room. I'm about to lower my face into it and breath it all in. But I stop.

I wait until evening, and I call your number that is on the business card in the bag. When you pick up, I say, "Talia Greenman? I have your suitcase. We must have been on the same flight."

You say, "Oh, um, who are you?" I am about to tell you my name when you add, "Goddamn it, *where are you?*"

BLISSFUL

Room 6 still smelled of Connie's lilac perfume an hour after she and Daryl had cleared out. Ellis could smell her in the shower when he scrubbed it down. The wastebasket bulged with beer cans and a pint bottle of schnapps with a trickle left in the bottom. That was Daryl's thing, the schnapps. Ellis figured that whenever Daryl brought her here overnight it was to heal some badness between them; he'd probably called in sick to work before driving her straight to the Hiscutt Motel. No damage done to the room, though—Ellis was supposed to check on that while cleaning. He leaned the vacuum against the desk, gulped the last sticky swallow of schnapps, stripped off his clothes and climbed into the bed, pulling the sheets up to his face, inhaling the lilac, feeling himself hardening in his fingers.

When he'd finished cleaning the room, he pushed the laundry cart across the parking lot toward Room 11. He saw George Hiscutt's flashlight blinking in the office window. Ellis ignored it; but when George rapped the butt-end of the light sharply on the glass, Ellis had to go in.

"You just did 6?" the old man asked. "They break anything in there?"

"Nope."

George looked almost disappointed. "Well, I think they did plenty of drinking there last night. It took you so long I thought they must have wrecked the place." Seated in his swivel chair, he folded his hands under his big belly like he needed to hold it from rolling away and dragging the rest of him with it. Ellis often thought he saw suspicion lurking in his boss's face when their eyes met. Suspicion of a Seneca Indian man with a homemade wooden cross hanging from his neck by a chain cut from a dog's leash.

"So, what's eating you now?" George asked.

"Nothing," Ellis said, forcing a grin.

He went out and pushed the cart across to a room that had just been vacated by a family. The sky was lusterless, chilly for June. At the desk in 11 he started a letter to Connie on motel stationary. Writing anything was hard for him, but writing to Connie was real work. Time to explain his love—to explain everything if he could. He crumpled up five sheets before turning to leaf through the silky insides of the Gideon Bible from the nightstand, looking for words that would make her sit up and think. Surprised he'd never thought of checking in there for love words before, being in the healing-business part time himself. The guys who wrote that book were real poets. God made them poets, even if they weren't when they started writing. *Behold I stand at the door and knock*, he scratched. *Be not wroth very sore. Love, Ellis Brown.*

He folded the letter and put it into a motel envelope and addressed it to Connie, licking a stamp he'd taken from the office right under George's nose. Then he walked to a mailbox on the corner, opened its jaws, and dropped it into the dark. Ellis had worked for George for six weeks before it came up that he'd done hard time in jail. He was running the vacuum in the office one day, and he offered to lay his healing hands on George's bloated feet and pray. George refused. "I don't want your hands on me, you'd probably get my wallet. Besides, the problem doesn't start in my feet, it's fluid from my heart." Ellis shrugged. Then George asked, "Where did you learn how to do your healing anyway? You ain't no preacher."

Ellis shut off the sweeper. He said he'd learned healing in prison, where he'd also found God.

"Prison?" George's big chin dropped. "For the Christ's sake, you should of told me you been in there."

Ellis expected George to fire him, but it didn't happen, probably because George could hardly walk on his own and needed him. But the old man took obvious precautions now. He always swiveled in his chair to face Ellis whenever the Seneca man came into his office. It aggravated Ellis to know that George was afraid he'd do something, like maybe slit his throat. Actually, Ellis wondered if he even had the capacity to kill. In prison, nightmares hounded him for months after he saw a man get a shiv in his back. The squirt gun he'd used to stick up a store—the deed that got him sent up—had leaked water all over his wrist and puddled on the counter right in front of the clerk he was threatening. He hollered, "I'll blow your fuckin' head off," then laughed and ran, later to be found sleeping in a junk Plymouth in the weeds behind his mother's house.

But when he came out from his nine-year stretch, the whole world seemed changed. He was back living with his mother in the house his father built on the Big Tree Reservation. But his mother's hair—charcoal when he went to jail—was white now, and she was thinner, almost brittle. His brother Russell—once a hell-raiser who claimed to have caught the clap four times in one summer—was married with kids, living in a double-wide on the more prosperous east end of the Res. Ellis's own hair was littered with gray, and he let it grow down to his collar. The wooden cross that hung from his neck was decorated, INRI, with hammered steel tacks. And Connie Crandall, red-haired white woman, was a good thirty-five or forty pounds heavier, the last woman he'd had before sentencing. So, she was extra now, *extra Connie*, and he wanted her that much more. He knew she had a thing for red men. God only knew what she'd been up to all the time he'd been away; married a couple times, he'd heard. But now she had Daryl Pickherd, a tall and gangly Seneca, a twelve-hour shift worker at the US Gypsum mine, who most nights dutifully left the Res at six for his job.

Ellis had left Attica Correctional Facility with nothing but the standard $40 release money, part of which paid his bus fare, and part for beer when he reached Hilford, five miles from Big Tree. Afraid to go home, he called his mother—relieved to find her still in the phone book—and blurted that he'd found the Lord in prison and learned faith healing. A complete lie, but he had to tell her he was different now. In fact, he told her, he could heal her too, in case anything was wrong with her. He could heal anybody. "You don't say," she said. "Come home and get some supper."

His last ten dollars paid for the taxi out the winding road to the house on the Res—where he found his aunt also waiting for him with a swollen knee, pulling up her skirt for him to lay his hands, sending him a scent he hadn't known for nine years. He was on the spot now, near panic. He knelt before her and called on God and wept, pleaded until his hands trembled and he could barely hold onto her lumpy arthritic bone. Then she sat back and looked at him, seeming to consider his shaking lips. "Praise the Lord," she said slowly.

Russell gave him an old car, and lent him $100. Later he regretted his generosity, and grumped about it when he came over to his mother's house where Ellis was staying. Russell, the big bear, with all his children and married pussy, didn't miss the cash—but he was the first to say that his brother was the same old Ellis with a new act, and he was sorry he'd helped finance it. Yet sick people came to him, even white people, and Ellis laid his hands on them and prayed.

Connie came to the Community House Dance on a Saturday with two other white girls she'd brought along for the adventure to see the Res and real Indians while she danced with Daryl. The white girls looked spooked to Ellis, though he danced with one, and everyone else ignored them politely. After Daryl left for work, Ellis danced with Connie. "You were the last piece I had before I went in the pen," he said as they slid clumsily around the band, and he felt her pulse between his fingers like a mouse's heart.

"No kidding," she said. "Get any while you were inside?"

Ellis followed Connie's path like a deer's. He stopped at Morgan's Tap Room on Friday after work. Connie sat alone out front in her old Pinto, a car that left an oily spoor from bar to bar, and had two giant dice hanging from her rearview mirror. A hard rain had just ended and the afternoon sun burned holes in the clouds and fried the beads of rain on her hood into vapor. She looked to be scowling at all creation. Must be waiting for Daryl, or maybe she just couldn't decide how bad she wanted to go inside. It was time for him to move. He yanked her car door open, got in on the passenger side and grabbed her arm. Lilac hit his nose again.

A what-the-hell look came over Connie, and her ears reddened.

He said, "Hey, I got something I been carrying around for you."

"You got something for me, huh?" Her lower lip protruded and he could see her gums. "Well, honey, I don't need nothing right now. Okay?"

"This thing you gotta have." From his shirt pocket he took a ring that he'd picked up that morning from his mother's dresser. He held it high for a moment like a host, then tried to jam it on the fat middle finger of Connie's right hand.

"Jesus, Ellis, where did you get this?" She yanked the

ring off from her first knuckle and held it up to squint at it.

"Bought it."

"You did? Well, God, I can't accept nothing like this. It looks like gold. I hardly even know you anymore. And don't look at me like that, neither."

"How do you want me to look?"

She peered straight into his eyes now, as if Ellis had just revealed himself to be an even stranger creature than she'd thought. "Ellis, this is childish. Don't try to give me this."

Meyer Potts, a middle-aged Seneca man, came out of the bar, grinned and patted the hood of Connie's car as he passed on his way to his truck. He didn't acknowledge Ellis. She tried to quickly open her car door, but he grabbed her arm again, and she looked scared now.

"Come on, put it on. Just put it on for an hour."

She clenched it in her fist, and rapped her knuckles lightly on her steering wheel as if this problem, the problem of Ellis, needed some thought. She smirked a little and looked at her watch. Finally she slipped it slowly onto her pink, smallest finger, the only one it would fit, dragging it over the joint—his mother's fingers were like willow twigs.

"Looks good, don't it?" he said. But she didn't answer. He wanted to say, *You're all I've thought about for nine fucking years in the pen.* Though it wasn't true. In fact, he hadn't come home thinking about her at all. But he'd started running into her again, noticing her giving him curious looks, and his old sleeping desire woke up, and he wanted her.

She popped open her door again and climbed out, walking quickly ahead of him through the barroom door like she was grabbing for safety inside. A half-dozen men were sitting around a table, and a couple of them hollered greetings to Connie. The look she gave Ellis now said, *See, you're not gonna act weird in here, mister, or your head's going on the end of a pole.* She settled her butt on a stool and ordered her first beer, spreading a five-dollar bill out on the bar, glancing nervously at him on the next stool. "Kaw-Liga" was playing on the jukebox. Ellis listened and twisted the remains of a peanut bag left on the bar.

Poor ol' Kaw-Liga, he never got a kiss.

Poor ol' Kaw-Liga, he don't know what he missed.

Connie talked, without really looking at him, mostly about what a crappy day she'd had, and suggesting that, thanks to him, it had taken a turn for the worst. How she hated her job answering the phone at the GMC truck dealership in Hilford, and typing up paperwork for salesmen she despised. "Ass-kissers, mostly." But she didn't seem completely satisfied with that term. "Suck-holes," she pronounced finally. It sounded to Ellis like a speech she'd been saving for Daryl, who hadn't shown up. So far.

She eyed the clock like it was something she wanted to eat. When six o'clock arrived, he knew Daryl wasn't coming, he wasn't calling in sick again to spend time with her. The few beers Ellis bought her then seemed to purchase friendliness. He wondered what she thought of his letter, and if she would ever let Daryl take her back to Hiscutt's after reading it.

"Tell me the trick, Ellis," she said. "How do you heal people?"

"Ain't no trick," he said. "It's God's work. I just touch sick people where they have a pain—head, arm, knee, wherever—and pray till I break out in a sweat." He looked at her. "Sometimes I sweat blood. Jesus did that when he prayed."

"Ick," she said. "You're a funny one to be doing that, anyway." She lit a cigarette and blew a cloud of smoke to the bottles on the back bar.

"Funny? How come you say that?"

"You're the last person I'd picture being a preacher."

"I ain't no preacher. Just a healer. I don't preach nothing."

She snorted. "I never knew there was a big difference."

Up close he saw features that he remembered from before prison: a fine little scar that divided her right eyebrow in two. Green speckled irises. Fingernails the color of deep blue water. He wanted to say to her again, *You're the last piece I had before prison.*

"You think it would work on my mother?" She looked away from him.

"Don't know. It don't work every single time. It's God's business whether it's gonna work or not. The sick person's gotta have faith in it. What's the matter with her?"

"Christ, everything's wrong with that old cow. You'd have to ask her what's tops on her list today. When I left this morning it was her heart again."

"Jesus knows what's wrong anyway. He can tell me where to lay my hands."

"Well, I wish somebody would do something for her and give me a break. Like I've got nothing else to do but look after her and wipe her ass. You know what I'm saying?"

He shrugged. "I can give it a try."

She looked at the ring on her little finger. "Now my finger's swelling up. I'm gonna have a bitch of a time getting this off." She looked at him again. "Who else you healed? Anybody I know?"

Ellis grinned. He had a list, all right. Though, other than Meyer Potts, few Senecas still came to him. He didn't know why, but he suspected rumors were going around the Res that maybe his healing didn't work. Maybe Russell was telling folks that. White people were still coming to him, though it didn't do him any good that he got booted out of a Pentecostal meeting in Hilford for stumbling in drunk. One white man, Nelson Ames, half crippled with arthritis, ran a gas station and used to fill Ellis's tank for free after healing sessions. But one day a preacher told Nelson that the healing wasn't God's work or the effect ought to be permanent. This business of having to get repeated treatments and put more gas in Ellis's car, well, the devil probably had his finger in that scheme. So, the next time Ellis pulled up to the pumps, Nelson limped out and, leaning his swollen elbows on the car window, stammered that he didn't need his help anymore and he told him why. Ellis could see Nelson's daughter standing a few paces behind him, and he knew she was there in case Ellis gave her father any guff.

"You saw Meyer outside? Well, he had the gout pretty good."

"So, you healed him? I thought gout goes away by itself."

"Not the way I did it. It was gone right then and there."

"Besides," Connie said after a swallow of beer, "he gets that all the time."

Ellis drove behind her, the blue-oily smoke from her Pinto making his eyes water. Connie and her mother lived in a farmhouse, well-kept until five years before when her father died from emphysema and her two sisters moved to Rochester. Then the weeds came creeping closer to the house as if they saw the old man was gone, and the barn leaned like somebody had tried to jerk the ground out from under it. But the house looked rich to Ellis. They had a washer and dryer in the big kitchen, and a second phone extension in the living room where Mrs. Crandall camped on the couch most of the time, her face giving a pale light like Ellis had seen in a few people, most beyond help, and who looked at him so desperately they gave him bad dreams.

Rolled up in an afghan, the old woman ignored Ellis when Connie introduced him. Instead, she turned up her radio. Connie brought her pills and a pitcher of ice water, and told her that Ellis was a faith healer, come to help her. Then the white woman looked at him like he'd just dropped from the clouds. But she said she didn't think she was worth his time.

"I don't expect to survive this humid summer anyway," she said. "This heat is trying to strangle me."

Ellis knelt and spread his hands on Mrs. Crandall's hips. He prayed and sang in a shrill that climbed the scale like a cat, repeating the name of Jesus until Connie left the room with her hands over her ears. But the old woman was rapt. He moved his hands to her shoulders then, and he kept up the wavering sing-song: *Jesus, Lord and Savior, send through me your blissful, heavenly healing power. And heal this poor old woman, dear Jesus.*

"I feel something, all right," she said. "A little better, I think. Maybe I'll never be perfect, but I feel a bit better."

Ellis sat back on the floor, wiping sweat from his face with his sleeve. The old woman was recounting her afflictions to him—asthma, constipation, gas, sinus, diabetes, fluttering heart—seeming to brighten with each detail.

Connie returned from the kitchen and stood looking at them. At last she asked her mother, "You feel like dinner?"

Mrs. Crandall gazed at her daughter. "I'm better, Connie."

"That's great, Mom," Connie answered, and Ellis turned to look at her because she sounded sullen. Maybe she expected her mother to be clicking her heels and dancing around her radio. Sometimes people expected that. People were stupid, but he couldn't hold that against them.

Ellis and Connie took the old woman's arms and supported her as she limped to the kitchen table. "Don't mention this to nobody," Mrs. Crandall said to Ellis. "My friends think this kind of thing is hokum, you know. They ought to try it sometime."

Rain fell again, leaving fog on the blue forget-me-nots in the weedy yard. They played cards and drank beer after supper and smoked cigarettes from Connie's pack. Connie told about a movie where a hillbilly did a terrible thing to another man while twisting his ear and telling him to squeal like a pig. "Connie," her mother's voice stiffened, "what kind of movie...?" Ellis also noticed the old woman's eyes were on the strange ring on her daughter's finger, but she said nothing about it.

After helping her mother upstairs to bed, Connie came back down and shot him a look of mock surprise. "Oh, I thought you'd of gone by now."

"Expect me to go back up the chimney after healing your mom?"

She dragged her teeth over her lower lip. "You can finish your beer, then I want to be by myself, okay?"

He watched her fill the sink with suds, while he drank and got another bottle from the fridge.

"Just help yourself, mister," Connie said and shot him an ugly look.

He laughed at her, prying off the cap while squinting one eye against the smoke of his cigarette.

"Hey," she said, "I got a question for you as long as you're here. You know who Flint was?"

"No, who the fuck was Flint?" What kind of trick was

this?

"Sh-h-h, don't use that language in the house," she said, turning back to the dishes. "Flint was...well, you see, I've been reading up on Seneca folk stories."

"What stories are you talking about?"

"I'm just interested, okay? Cause I've been going out with Daryl. I went to the library looking for a book on Indian stuff and I found these Seneca stories."

Ellis laughed. "White people always want to hear the Indian stories. You ought to wear buckskins when you read that book."

"You say nobody ever told you about a man named Flint when you was a kid?"

"Sounds like the fucking boogieman. Besides, I hardly knew I was an Indian when I was a kid. All knew for sure was—"

"Ellis, I'm telling you. My mom's gotta hear you swearing all the way up the stairs. You ain't in no bar. So watch your mouth and gums."

"Okay. Sorry." He gazed at the stretched jeans across her buttocks, and the line of her bra under the back of her blouse, tight as a towrope.

"Anyway, there's this one story about the first brothers on earth, Sapling and Flint." She set wet dishes in the drainer. "Sapling was good, but Flint was a thief and a murderer. His mother even died giving him birth because he was born through her armpit. Flint was the cause of—"

"Bullshit," Ellis said. "The first brothers on earth was Cain and Abel. That's a fact. The scientists even dug up their bones."

"Yeah, you know your Bible real good. But this is just a story, okay?" She rinsed a handful of silverware.

"I ain't no murderer, and no thief neither. If that's what you're trying to get at."

"I never said you were. It's just a story. You're wild though."

He laughed. "Well, I like to have a few beers, but I don't make no trouble. The troublemakers are the people that don't answer letters."

He stood up and stroked her back and, pushing his nose through her hair, kissed the back of her neck. She turned around and, barely touching his shoulders with her wet hands, kissed his mouth. Dishwater soaked his arm and made him curse again, only quietly now. *That's it,* she told him. *If you gotta swear, do it quiet. Whatever you do around here you do it quiet as possible.* She pulled him away by his arm to a room near the kitchen. He stumbled on a curled edge of linoleum going in and went down on one knee. A glossy poster of a movie star stared him in the face as she shut the door.

"Who the hell's that?"

She gave him an incredulous look. "Charles Bronson. Where you been?"

"You know where the hell I been."

She let him study the photo for a minute before she turned off the light.

Making love to Connie wasn't like he remembered from before he got sent up. This time she made no moans, didn't draw blood from his shoulder with her teeth, didn't ribbon his back with her fingernails. Maybe the old Connie still lived somewhere inside this big woman, and he just couldn't thrust deep enough to reach her and wake her up. Though he pushed until he thought the bed would break. Lying awake hours later he remembered she'd told him to get out of the house before daylight, or her mother would raise hell. Her green clock glowed 2:23, and Connie wasn't stirring. Hadn't stirred in a long time. He wanted to go, come back after he'd gotten some solid sleep. A hangover lurked in his blood, trying to take possession of his head and stomach, and he wondered how much he'd drank during the day and the past evening.

Crawling on the floor in the dark, he gathered his clothes and shoes. He dressed next to the bed, watching Connie, how her big body sank into the sheets and made her look small from above. He took his cross from where he'd hung it on her doorknob and slipped it around his neck again. As he buckled his belt, her hand shot out to him, putting something in his palm before he could think. He felt the warm ring in his fingers.

Stunned, he said, "How come you're giving me this?"

"Sh-h-h-h-h-h! Quiet, will you? I can't wear no ring of yours."

"Why the hell not?"

"Because I'm marrying Daryl."

"Daryl? Bullshit."

"Quiet down, you crazy Indian. Go ask him yourself if you don't believe me."

"Then what did you bring me over here for?"

"To heal my mother, you creep. Will you shut up now before you wake her up?"

"You fucking whore," he snarled, pulling down the poster of Charles Bronson, ripping it in two and four, and throwing the pieces on her.

Shrieking, she leaped from bed, slapping him. He blocked the blows that followed, stumbling on the linoleum again, backing away from her into the kitchen. Connie bore down on him, naked, slapping at his shoulders and head. It would be over in a minute, he thought. She would stop. But she didn't. She was a pot boiling over. Confused, he stumbled out the kitchen door. He leaned against his dew-covered car, staring at her looming form in the doorway, round and white. Getting behind the wheel, he started the engine, made it roar, then joined the gears. His tires kicked up great wigs of sod as he fishtailed through the yard and the forget-me-nots, bounced over the stones of a fallow flowerbed, and out onto the moonlit road.

He woke on the couch to the commotion of his mother turning over cushions, shaking out drawers. He knew what this must be about. Nauseous, he searched his pockets for the ring and realized he must have dropped it in Connie's house during the melee. He sat up and ran his fingers through his hair. Maybe he should go back for it. But no, better to let things settle down there. His mother quizzed him until he finally stood up, muttering, "How the hell should I know where your ring is?" He went out to the front yard where Russell was digging a posthole for his mother's new mailbox. His brother often came over Saturday mornings to play fix-it man around his mother's house. Ellis knew Russell suspected him of knocking over the old mailbox with his car a few days before, but that was one thing he knew for sure he didn't do.

"Cripe, you stink of beer," Russell snorted. "Unless you want to help me fix this mess, go breathe somewhere else."

Stalking away, Ellis said, "Go to hell," to his brother,

who ignored him and went on digging.

He searched his car, under the seats, under the floor mats, and the glove compartment. If he found the ring, he would put it in some silly place like the refrigerator, wait for his mother to find it and then accuse her of sleepwalking and putting it there herself. Make her laugh. But the ring wasn't in the car.

Instead he coaxed five dollars from her, added it to the two singles in his pocket, and drove into town for a pint of whiskey. His gas needle told him that he might not make it home again if he spent all the money on a pint. After leaving the liquor store with twenty-three cents change, and his gauge on E, he cut over to Reese Street and pulled up to Nelson Ames' pumps. Maybe the old guy had wised up by now and wanted some relief from his arthritis in exchange for gas, even just a couple gallons. Or one gallon. The same teenage girl he'd seen the last time he stopped came out of the office and stood with her fingers in the pockets of her jeans.

"Nelson around?" Ellis asked.

"My dad? He doesn't work here anymore." Her eyes seemed to measure the distance between them, and the threat level. Her hands were greasy, and one knuckle was bloody. But otherwise she didn't look much like Nelson, and that was her good luck.

"How come? Where'd he go?"

"He had a heart attack," she answered with a shrug, taking the nozzle off the pump and holding it up expectantly.

"Too bad." The last full service station in town, last place you had any hope of making a bargain.

"Yeah, me and my mom run the place now. Dad just does the bookkeeping."

Ellis gave her his twenty-three cents, and she laughed as she pumped it with one squeeze of the nozzle and a couple of jogs. She carried the money inside, and he saw her watching as he drove away. Two blocks down the street he veered into the Hiscutt Motel, coasting to a stop in front of the office. A little advance from George would help, even five bucks. In fact, the old bastard owed him for two weeks and ought be able to fork over that much. But before he could open the door he saw the flashlight blinking furiously in the window, like an alarm going off. Must have a lot of dirty sheets to wash. Or somebody puked in one of the rooms, or flushed a towel down a toilet and plugged it up. He laughed at the light, jamming his car into reverse. His fuel needle dropped a little more.

Back on the road to the Res he saw a car weaving behind him like its driver was drunk and trying to drive over the top of him. Then he recognized the blue replacement hood of Daryl's red Fairlane, though the sight of Daryl himself was blotted by an orb of sun-glare burning in the windshield like a big devil chasing him. The car shifted and careened as Daryl laid on his horn and tried to squeeze around each side of him. But Ellis kept his speed low and held the middle of the narrow blacktop, hunkering down in the seat. He knew Daryl would shove him into a tree if he could get beside him. For the first time he was really afraid of the man, whom he'd have rather faced with fists or sticks or anything but his car diving down on him. The Fairlane hit his rear bumper like a bull in heat, jerking his neck and springing his trunk lid, leaving it flapping. *Keep pushing,* Ellis muttered as they crossed the line onto the Res, *'cause I'm almost out of gas.* Sweat ran down his back and heartburn boiled in his throat.

At last he skidded into his mother's yard, tearing up grass. Ellis got out and looked around quickly for Russell, but his brother had apparently abandoned his digging project for lunch, leaving the shovel in the dirt. Daryl leaped out of his car, holding the ring up in his hand. So, he'd been to Connie's already this morning. When Daryl grabbed his shirt, Ellis caught a strong whiff of schnapps. He yanked himself loose from Daryl, ripping his shirt, and strode to the rear of his car, running his hand over the damage. "Dumb son-of-a-bitch," he said. Green coolant hissed through the front grill of the Fairlane, and the vapor stung Ellis's eyes. His neck ached from the jolts.

"Trying to screw my old lady?" Daryl started.

"Huh? Trying to?" Ellis smiled. "It was easy. I forgot how many times, though."

Daryl grabbed at him again, but Ellis dodged and snatched the shovel from the dirt, brandishing it almost comically like a batter. But Daryl still came at him, like in a dream. He struck Daryl across his ribs with the edge of the spade, who gave a big *Whoof*, stumbled backward and knelt in the road, hugging himself with his arms, coughing and bowing his face to the pavement. Ellis watched, holding the trembling shovel above his head. It looked like Daryl was laughing, though Ellis knew that couldn't be true. This wasn't funny. He said something that Ellis couldn't hear.

"What are you saying?" Ellis stepped closer. "What's that I hear?"

"I can't breathe."

"You can't? Then how come you can talk?" He grinned. "I can't talk when I ain't breathing. What's your secret?"

Ellis stepped back again. Maybe Daryl was faking, would suddenly leap and strike. But then he vomited, gagged and spat a couple times on the pavement, and slumped again in a denim heap. Ellis flung the shovel into the middle of the yard, and strode into the house under the wild gaze of his mother and sister Marcie who was visiting for lunch.

"He's okay," he said in answer to both of them. "Just a little cool around the gills." He sat at the kitchen table, taking a long draw from his pint. But he guessed there was no time for leisurely drinking.

His mother walked out to the road and knelt, touching Daryl's shoulder, picking up her ring from the pavement. She hollered for Russell. Ellis heard his brother stirring from the living room couch, grumbling, "What's going on?" Then everyone was running like there was a fire. Marcie dragged her daughter Louise up to bed in her grandmother's room, the girl screaming all the way that it wasn't time for bed, she'd just had lunch, and she wanted to see what that man was doing lying down in the road.

If he hadn't panicked he could have taken his car, and maybe the little gas he had would have gotten him off to a better run. Off the Res, at least. He ran until he felt the whiskey begin to leaden his blood, slowing him to a walk on an uphill stretch of woods. He leaned against a tree for a few minutes until his stomach settled. Dripping wet, he smelled to himself like a sour dishrag. He took another swallow of whiskey, then he started moving again. The growl of a motorcycle on the road told him that Daryl's brother LaVerne must have joined the hunt along with the cops, although he hadn't heard a siren. When night fell he

prayed on his knees, although it frightened him to close his eyes. He reminded God that no one ever healed Ellis Brown. *No one ever did jack for me.* Yet he didn't know what to ask for now that had any chance of coming true. When he came to his mother's road for the second time that night, he realized his escape had been one continuous circle.

In the morning he woke in the back seat of the old Plymouth—the dead, wheelless shell behind the house, exactly where he had been found nine years before. He had come to it in the night this time, crawling in through an open window, figuring someone would be watching for him at the house and would hear him if he opened the rusty car door. Maybe even shoot him. A protruding seat spring jabbed him between his loose shirt and belt. Years of weather-blown seeds and twigs littered the seats and floor.

But it was a sound that woke him—feet approaching through the weeds as morning light glittered in the windshield. And in a moment he saw his mother's face and white hair. She knocked on the car with her small fist. Ellis sat up and climbed out of the car without a word. She immediately locked her arm with her son—just like nine years ago. Frail and skinny, she steadied him. She must have talked the troopers into treating him kindly, like she did before. She'd said, *I'll go see if he's hiding out back, just don't hurt him*. He asked her if Daryl was dead. And what the police had said.

"What police are you talking about?"

He only looked at her. He couldn't take his eyes off hers, though he wanted to.

"No," she continued, "Daryl isn't dead. For heaven's sake." He was home recuperating in bed. She had just come from there herself, getting the whole story straight. And Daryl ought to be whipped for what he tried to do.

He put his face on her shoulder and his cross knocked against her ribs.

"Now," she said, "I've got a bone to pick with you about that ring. I'm *considering* calling the police. There's a whole list of things you've stolen off me since you got out of the pen. I've been keeping track. Writing them all down. I'll bet you didn't know I was doing that. Did you?"

"No," he wept on her boney shoulder.

"You want me to show it to you?"

"No."

"What do you think I ought to do?"

"What do you mean?" he sobbed.

"Should I call the police and have you put in jail again so you can't keep stealing off me the few precious things I own?"

It occurred to him now that he had never healed his mother of anything, any ailment. There had never been a need because she never complained. He lifted his face from her shoulder, and the morning sun made him feel naked. Wild grapevine and nightshade hung coolly from the trees. His mother's windows looked black and empty as if no one lived there. As if he saw the future when she was years dead.

"Sure. Yeah."

"What? Sure-yeah what?"

"Call the cops," he sobbed.

She sighed and said, "Let's get on into the house."

They walked slowly, the dewy weeds soaking their shoes. Out in front of the house, by the porch, he stopped short, seeing the old Pinto sitting in the driveway with Connie's big dice hanging from the mirror. He couldn't look at it now. The puddling of oil and coolant under the engine nauseated him.

His mother said, "I guess I ought to be glad you ain't on drugs. As far as I know."

They mounted the porch steps and entered the house. Connie sat at the kitchen table in a blue skirt, her face swollen from crying and eyes red. Her lilac filled the air. Turning his head away, he told her he was sorry. Might as well apologize to her and everybody else, he thought. One after another, and get it over with.

"My mother's worse," she said.

Her statement confused him for a moment. Was he to blame for that too? "Well, take her to a doctor."

Connie stomped her foot. "She won't go. Ellis, this is different than before. I'm scared."

"Call an ambulance or something."

Connie shook her head. "She thinks if she goes, she'll never come home again. She thinks I'm trying to get rid of her."

He strode past her into the bathroom and splashed cold water on his face.

Connie drove. All the way he held his stomach, sweating, watching her steer with a cigarette tucked in her grip on the wheel. He told her he used to think he knew what he was doing when he laid healing hands on people. "I used to think it was God's power helping me. But I don't know no more. You know what I mean? So now I'm figuring out that I gotta be humble. That's the whole thing right now. Healing might be everybody's goddamned imagination, anyway. I don't even know if God knows who the hell I am."

"Okay, Ellis, shut up already. If you won't do it, just say so. But I'll never speak to you again."

"I don't know if I can or I can't. That's all I'm saying. How do I know? Told you, I'm humble now. I learned something."

"Learned something how? Drinking and screwing and hitting Daryl with a shovel? You want to go over to his house and look at his ribs?"

He shook his head.

She scowled. "Well, he asked for it that time. The dumb ass."

The ruts in Connie's yard looked worse than he expected, like someone went berserk on a tractor. He thought of apologizing for that too, but decided it was best not to bring it up. Following her inside, he could hear a radio droning. The old lady's face looked ashen in her sleep, as if a frost had taken her soul away. Was she already dead?

"Mom," Connie spoke, and the old woman opened her eyes, confused at first, then recognizing the two faces in the room.

"Oh," she said to Ellis, "you'll have to come down here and do your business. I can't set up right now."

Ellis knelt by the couch, his knees paining him. He drew a deep breath and he placed his hands on the woman's heart. And he prayed. He hollered and strained an entreaty to God with all his strength until he thought his voice would snap. He asked forgiveness for himself to make sure he was clean and fit to perform this healing—in case he had done anything lately that was a 'bomination in God's sight. His shoulders trembled when he felt a flood of power coming finally. God was with him. It rushed from his breast down his arms so hot and fluid that it terrified him, through his hands and into the old woman like the giving of blood. His lips wept spit, his face dripped sweat. And he knew he was forgiven and blessed with the blissful healing Gift of the Holy Spirit. Ellis prayed ever harder for her now, with all his might until finally he felt himself break like a stick and collapse in soft tears.

He heard the woman sit up, slowly, as his forehead came to rest on the floor beside her slippers. She said, "That wasn't as good as last time. But I feel some better." Then she yelled, "Connie." And her daughter came from the kitchen. "Help me to the table, please. Both of you. Help me."

"Mom, are you okay?" Connie whispered.

Ellis struggled to his feet, and held Mrs. Crandall's arm in his.

They ate a lunch of hot dogs and canned macaroni. They smoked cigarettes and played cards. Connie didn't get after him to leave this time. When Ellis asked for a drink, she went to the cupboard and returned with a quart of schnapps. "I've been saving this for something," she said. "I don't remember what."

IT JUST SO HAPPENED

I knew a woman who had a black helicopter, an army surplus from about six wars ago. Her name was Roberta, and she inherited the copter from her father. He was a nut beyond classification, and yet, beside the people I'm going to tell you about, Roberta's father wouldn't stand out. She was an insurance agent, and she used the helicopter for what she called her side work. She contracted it out for Mercy Flights for the severely injured. Helped police hunt criminals in the woods. That sort of thing. Once she airlifted a rock band out of a stadium after the crowd found out they were lip-syncing and went berserk en-masse. The whirly bird's original color was probably kiwi or steel blue. She didn't know why her father painted it black, but she also belonged to a club of people that flew black aircraft of all descriptions. Some of the members, she admitted, were weird.

I met Roberta when she came to my door to personally apologize for sending the cops into the woods to pop me after she saw me from the air, wandering through the trees.

She'd thought I was the murderer they were looking for. I was actually an innocent hiker on my way to harvest a crop of weed I had growing a couple miles down the ravine. The guy they were really after was a major bad-ass, had shot three guys in a barroom brawl, and was a suspect in a catalog of other dirt. So, they landed on me hard, coming out of the trees and bushes on all sides. I got bruised up pretty bad that morning, and I had big trouble convincing the cops of who I was and who I wasn't, because I'd lost my driver's license a year before and had no picture ID. But I counted myself lucky that they grabbed me before I got to my weed patch.

The killer's name was Gaylord Mosby, and he'd been in the papers for three days. His cousin had told a reporter some intimate details, that Mosby's father had twisted the boy's brain before he was even ten years old. He'd got drunk one Sunday and tied the boy to a post, pulled his pants down and sizzle-branded the cheek of his ass with the logo of his two-bit ranch. I brought this fact up to the cops while they were interrogating me, and a sudden glimmer bounced like a firefly from one cop's face to another. They shoved me down face-first on a table and yanked down my drawers. Found nothing but a few freckles and a rash.

Even then I wasn't sure they were going to let me go. They shoved me back in my chair, my pants still around my ankles, and the meanest one said, "Then what *were* you doing in the woods, Mr. Duckworth?"

"It's state park land, goddamn it. I was going for a picnic."

To be honest, I had the hots for Roberta, but she was older than me by ten years, and a half-foot taller. We made friends anyway, and she took me up with her in the helicopter on one of her Mercy Flights. Same stadium, and another rock concert, only this time we were airlifting a pregnant teenager whose water had broken. We were just in time. Once we had her aboard, I tried to stay out of the way of the EMTs, but I witnessed the birth of probably the only baby in the world born while flying in a black helicopter while ten thousand people below, including Dickey Betts and the Great Southern Band, hooted their happy wishes.

By that time a woman named Clea was deep in my life. I met her at the police station the day they were interrogating me for the murders. She was in for plain old shoplifting, and at one point we were sitting on a bench together. They were getting ready to drive me home, and she was waiting to get thrown in a holding cell. A big female cop had just come by and patted her down for about the seventh time, but this time she smiled at Clea and told her that she'd just been on the phone to the store and the value of all the watches she'd heisted came to only $995—five bucks short of grand larceny. "You're a lucky girl," she said as she lumbered away.

Clea looked at me and said, "What'd they get you for?"

"Hiking," I said.

"Geez, everything's illegal now."

I said, "Yeah, just about."

"I'm beginning to see what my daddy means about all that stuff."

A cop came into the room swinging his car keys, and hollered, "Come on Duckworth, let's go home."

But I wanted her to finish her thought. "What does your daddy say?"

"Oh, you know, the whole apocalypse thing about the locusts and the black helicopters. That stuff."

The cop hollered, "Leave the prisoner alone, Duckworth."

But we managed to exchange emails before the cop boiled over completely. Her daddy bailed her out later that day, telling her to plead innocent. But it was no good, she'd confessed hours before while they still had her in the back of the patrol car. And anyway, her purse was stuffed with the watches.

I've got to describe her daddy for you. Gray headed and lanky and six-feet ten, or thereabouts. They never had his jeans size at Walmart, so he bought the longest ones they had and then his wife Trina would sew an extension on the cuffs with whatever material they had around the house, like old couch upholstery. His face was blotchy red all the time—I don't know what that signified but it wasn't serenity. He was always challenging me to a boxing match, but his arms were a yard long and I didn't have a chance. Oh, that was another thing, Walmart didn't have his shirt sizes either so Trina sewed the same kind of extensions on his sleeves. He'd have a denim work shirt and about eight inches of beige curtain fabric for cuffs. Another shirt had one red cuff and one blue.

It wasn't easy dating Clea. I mean, I knew from the get-go that she had a problem, and all my inner voices were saying, *Leave her alone, Duckworth.* Everywhere we went she had her sticky fingers out, stuffing something in her coat, and I was always afraid we'd get pulled over on the road and shook down by the cops. I saw us sitting handcuffed on a guardrail while they riffle through my car, throwing all sorts of merchandise out on the road that I didn't know about: diamond bracelets, silk bras, and a couple dozen DVDs still in their wrappers. And the big woman cop patting us both down, spending a little extra time on Clea. Plus, they'd throw the book at me for driving without a license. As far as I knew, Clea never stole anything out of my apartment, but the stuff she gave me had to be hot, like the ebony hash pipe. On my birthday she brought over a bottle of wine, a French Margaux 1958, and she said, "I don't know nothing about wine. You think this stuff is good?"

I don't want to sound like we weren't good together, because we were, most of the time. I mean, I felt a level of tenderness I'd never felt before. And after all, she was red-haired and willowy. But more than that, she was the kind of woman who'd look sexy if she was wearing Chairman Mao's suit and shoes. I knew I had to either live with all the pilfering, or else tell her to stop it cold if she wanted me to stick around. I was in love and riding passion's white water. But every once in a while, out of the blue, she'd say something like, "See you next week, Mr. Duck."

And I'd say, "What do you mean, next week? What's the matter with this coming Saturday?"

"Dad's got the black bug up his ass again."

That meant he was having another one of his paranoid spells where he was seeing federal agents watching him from the trees, and he thought all human civilization was about to collapse. He'd load his armored jeep up with guns and food. Then he and Trina—a fiery woman, though she only came up to about the bottom of his rib cage—and *my dear Clea,* would head for an underground shelter they had up in the hills some place. I didn't know where, but I figured it must have been out in the pine hills where the cops had wrestled me to the ground and poked a gun up the crack of my ass. In a few days, or maybe four or five, they'd be back home and he'd be working in his barn or his metal shop like nothing had ever happened.

But whenever they went away it was like a curtain fell between me and Clea. And it always took a while after she came back for things to feel good again, partly because she wouldn't talk about it. I mean, I wanted to know what the hell they were doing out there all that time. But since she had at least some fear that her daddy was right, it meant that she was leaving me out of her post-apocalyptic future. Like, fuck you and good luck with the Beast. I can't honestly say I wanted to go—imagine getting stuck in some underground bunker with that seven-foot lunatic wanting to box with everybody. But I couldn't get over what leaving me out meant to her. I was boiling into a jealous stupor.

So, it was during one of those family-style self-raptures that I went to Roberta. Reason told me that if Harry was really seeing black helicopters, it was probably Roberta doing a Mercy Flight, or helping the cops find some major badass. But now I was ready to pay her my hard-earned money to find out where they were holing up.

"Hell," she said, "I can find a kitty cat in those woods." She was sitting in her swivel chair in her little insurance office in her house.

I said, "What makes you think I'm talking about the woods?"

She put one of her blood-red cowboy boots up on her desk. "Well," she said, and dawdled a moment like she was deciding whether she was really going to tell me or not. "Out there in the pine hills, in the state park land, not as far east as your marijuana patch—"

I was thunder-struck that she knew about that, but she held up a hand to shush me.

"—but west of there, and a little north, there's a bunch of squatters. I don't know how many. There's Vietnam shell-shocked vets that disappeared into those hills in the late '60s, early '70s, and never came out again except to sell their rutabagas, or whatever they got, and buy ammunition. They don't bother anybody, and some of them are starting to die off. They sure don't buy insurance. And then there's the other more recent ones, survivalists, I guess. They're political and they're dangerous. All of them are in about a thirty square-mile area. I'll bet my grandma's under panties that's where they are. You want to have a look?"

An hour later we were lifting off from a little private

airport at the edge of town. Roberta said it was getting harder to get parts for the old whirly bird, and it needed a new hydraulic fluid reservoir, and if she couldn't get that and a few other parts she needed at a reasonable price she was going to have to sell it to some rich collector. "Besides," she said, "I'm losing a lot of sleep with all these Mercy Flights. Last night I was carrying a farmer with a crushed head. His son ran over his bean with the hay wagon. The old man wouldn't shut up neither, though he was mostly talking through the side of his skull and I couldn't understand what the hell he was saying. Try getting to sleep after something like that."

As we swept over the pine hills, she said, "So, who is this Clea? What's her last name?"

"Heffernan."

"Uh-*huh*." She repeated the name over and over, like she was tossing a ball up and down in her hand. Then she shook her head. "I know most of these outposts. They've dug them into the earth and tried to camouflage them with brush, but I can see them from a thousand feet in the air."

Roberta handed me her binoculars and told me to look for anything suspicious. "You should see some little mounds in the hillsides." Then she added, "Wait a minute," and she took the glasses back. She looked through them and said, "That one down there's a relatively new one. Least, I didn't see it last time I came up this way."

I tried to follow where she was pointing, but all I saw were scrubby pines and brush. When she dropped down about five hundred feet, I saw it, a real door in the hillside and a couple ventilator stacks poking up through the brush. If the Heffernans were trying to hide, they weren't doing a very good job. In fact, I could see the jeep under a camouflage of branches.

Roberta was still looking through her glasses, and she said, "Yep, that's him. Harry Heffernan himself. Walking around. He hears us but he can't see us, 'cause the sun's in his eyes." She chuckled.

"How do you know her father?"

"Old Harry? God. Cops have been watching his creepy ass for a long time. I've gone and hung this birdie over his house any number of nights trying to figure out—"

"Figure out what?"

"*Whoop*, look out, he's got a gun."

We lifted up about a thousand feet before he fired his first shot. Most of the shots missed us, but I heard a couple whap-whaps on the underbelly of the bird. We lifted higher.

"Looks like an AK he's got there. Not very accurate beyond three hundred yards, but I'm not taking any chances." A minute later she said, "He's reloading. The crazy son of a bitch."

We drew away then in a long sweep back across the hills, and when we were safely out of range, Roberta got on the radio to the state police. And when I tried to stop her, she put her big hand in my face and pushed me back in my seat.

The State Police SWAT team stormed the Heffernans' bunker. Besides the Heffernans themselves, they found enough weapons and ammunition to arm a revolution, and enough stolen merchandise, diamonds, gold, rubies, Rolexes, necklaces, bangles and earrings to fund a new nation. I swear, even a couple vases from Pharaonic Egypt. And cases of Q-Tips—what the hell did they want those for? Oh, I forgot the bombs—enough to blow the new nation away again. Harry took most of the rap, because he tried to shoot it out with the cops, and he got a stretch long enough to last into the hereafter. I always wondered if they had to make special prison clothes to fit him. Mom was charged with being an accessory, but a public defender got her off with misdemeanor resisting arrest, and she walked out of the can after a week. The same lawyer got Clea's rap for possession of stolen property reduced to ninety days by arguing that the old man was the real bad dog in the family.

But I was in a bad place too, alone with myself—me who'd gotten his girlfriend and her whole family busted and her father sent up for the big stretch. I wondered if Clea knew I'd dropped the dime. Wouldn't her lawyer know all the circumstances surrounding the raid and arrests, and wouldn't he share that information with her? She must be sitting in her cell imagining all the ways she'd kill me, and drag my body behind her car until nothing was left of me but a shin bone bumping along on the end of a rope. Though I suppose the cops keep snitchers confidential. I told myself all the reasons why it wasn't my fault, that the Heffernans did it to themselves. But down in my guts it didn't work. I had an urge bucking like a horse inside of me to commit a violent crime and get myself sent up. Just to atone. Rob a super market, and instead of running, sit on the floor and count the bills until the cops show up with their guns drawn. But my balls weren't made out of that kind of metal.

It just so happened one morning I got a call at work. "Ducky? Is that you? Duck-Duck?" It was Clea. "You gonna come and pick me up this morning?"

I stumbled. "What? Where?"

"At the pen, stupid. I've already been processed out and I'm sitting on a bench like a can of cigarette butts."

I made excuses at work about a family situation, and headed for the county lockup, my stomach knotting like a greasy fist.

"Don't tell me why you didn't write to me," she said when she was in the car and I was pulling out onto the highway. "*Or visit.* You don't have an alibi worth listening to. I'll bet you don't got any smoke in the car neither, right?"

I wanted to get the jail out of my rearview mirror before I discussed smoke, like I was afraid we could get sucked backward into its hungry hatch.

"Under your seat, where it always is," I told her.

She found the bag and rolled a joint the size of one of Harry's thumbs. "Can I keep half an ounce?" she said, looking contrite. "I mean, I'm just sprung this morning and I ain't got nothing."

I told her to keep the whole bag. It might have been two or three ounces, a fraction of what I'd harvested over the summer. We were sailing down her road now, smoking and feeling weightless, and listening to Dylan sing "Knocking on Heaven's Door." When we pulled into her muddy yard, her mother came running out to hug and kiss and cry over her. Hovering behind like a shadow was some guy dressed in her father's work pants. He was a good foot and a half shorter than old Harry, and even leaner, so that the pant legs were rolled up a dozen times. He had thin sandy hair and a pair of sideburns that were so long they almost joined above his Adam's apple. He shook hands with me without asking my name, and I didn't ask his. We all went into the house.

Drinks all around. Her mother sipping whiskey while Clea and this odd other man drank beer. He was watching me watching Clea, who, far from the serene woman I arrived with, was wired now, agitated, and never sat down. She turned the TV on, then surfed through the channels and turned it off again. For once I didn't want anything to drink. Her mom said, "Staying for supper, Ducky?"

I said I guessed so, and thanks. But a wariness was puddling in my belly when I looked at the man.

He got up from the couch and waved to me to follow him. "Come on, Champ," he said. He didn't wait for me but walked down a hall to the back door. I got up and followed. It was a door I'd never been through before.

When we were outside I said, "My name isn't Champ."

But he didn't seem to hear me. He said, "We got to grab a chicken."

We stopped in the barn where he opened a bin and took a handful of chicken feed and we went around to the back where the chickens were penned in. He threw the hens the handful of feed, and they went for it. A rooster stood on top of a random pile of boards in the far end. The man pulled a pistol from his pants, and shot the rooster's head off. The hens went bonkers.

I said, "Looks like they've only got one rooster. Did you

have to shoot him?"

He nodded at the heap of chicken on the pile of boards. "Go and get it."

"I'm not your golden retriever."

"Afraid of getting a little chicken blood on your hands?"

"What the hell is this all about?"

He looked at me like I'd insulted him right to the bone, and the tendons stood out on his neck. "This is about getting a chicken for dinner. Besides, eggs from chickens that fuck give me the creeps. How hard is that to understand?" Now his face morphed slowly into a grin. "I looked after the place while Clea and Trina were in the pen." He put the gun back in his pants. "What's your claim to fame?"

"None," I said.

"Sorry, I didn't mean to piss on you. I'm just practicing what I'm gonna do when I find the sonofabitch that blew in the whole Heffernan family." He went into the chicken pen and picked the rooster up by its leg.

Clea was fussing with the TV again when I came in the house. She gave me a bewildered look. "Did Gaylord just shoot a chicken?"

Gaylord? The murderer with the brand on his ass? "Yeah," I said, "your rooster."

Trina heard me and bolted into the living room from the kitchen. "Did I hear you right? That *moron* shot Mr.

X?"

I said, "I guess he'll have to service those hens himself."

Clea thought that was funny. Trina scowled and went back to her stove.

After dinner we were all drinking and playing cards, and smoking from the stash I'd given Clea. Trina didn't smoke, but she got good and drunk and she wept from time to time. She said she wished Daddy was home to welcome Clea. She wished Daddy was home, *period*. She said that the chair that Gaylord was sitting in was Harry's, where he always sat. Clea didn't know what to say, I guess, so she just kept quiet while her mother blubbered on.

Then Trina jerked her head up at the ceiling. "Oh God," she shouted, standing up.

"What?" Clea said, startled.

Trina sat back down and buried her face in her hands. "I'm sorry, it's just the freezer kicking on. I could of sworn I heard that helicopter again."

Gaylord twirled his gun on his finger and rhapsodized about what he was going to do the motherfucker who did the deed.

Trina dropped her hands and stared at Gaylord like he was a dog turd on the rug. Her voice went taut as a guywire. "Young man, we don't use language like that around this house. Ever."

Clea went eyes-wide. "Mommy, don't."

"And while we're talking," Trina added, her voice rising, "you put that gun away the rest of the time you're under this roof."

"Mommy, just skip it."

When Trina started to get up out of her chair, a confused look washed over Gaylord's face. He still had the gun in his lap.

Trina said, "If there's any more shooting to be done around here, I'm going to do it."

That seemed to settle things. Gaylord stuffed the gun in one of the big pockets in his pants, and I was glad as hell to see it gone.

Clea said to me, "What was that song we was listening to on the way over here?"

I said, "Knocking on Heaven's Door."

"That's it." She sang, "'Mama put my guns in the ground. I can't shoot them anymore. That long black helicopter's coming down.'"

"It's 'long black cloud,'" I said.

"Yeah, I know, but I'd rather sing long black helicopter."

Now Trina was standing, teetering, aiming a hatchet look at Gaylord. "I never said you could wear Daddy's pants."

He looked shocked, and stammered, "Well, I didn't have nothing else to wear."

"Where's the clothes you wore over here in the first place?"

"You put them in the goddamn washing machine. That's where they still are."

"Bullshit. The very day I came home from the pen I saw you're walking around with Daddy's shoes on. His pants too. You got his underpants on?"

Clea pleaded, "Mommy, I just got home myself. Don't start this now."

"I think..." Trina wavered, and Clea reached to steady her. "I think all my sus . . ." she stammered, and finally shouted, "*suspicions*...are a bull's eye." She knocked her drink over.

Gaylord scraped his chair back from the table. "What're you getting all suspicious about *now*?"

"You wearing all Daddy's clothes. And all this time you're the one called the cops."

The man stood. He pulled the gun out of his pants and set it on the table. "Lady, I'll take it all off right here and now." He was drunk too, and his tendons were popping again. Then an afterthought hit him, and he picked up the gun again and aimed it at Trina. "You take yours off, first."

She said, "You really would shoot me. You really, really

would," and she sat down again, trying to hold her sobs inside her face like cats squirming in a bag .

That was when I figured out that this was a lovers' wrangle. I said, "Well look, why don't you shoot me? I'm the one that blew you all in to the police. You can take turns blasting me."

They all stopped and looked at me, eyes wide as if a goat had come in out of the barn and took a seat at the table. I smiled.

Gaylord said, "Yeah, like hell you did."

Trina sat back in her chair and let out a sound, like crying at first, then it straightened itself out into a laugh. She grabbed Gaylord's gun just as he set it down again. She stood teetering, hollow faced, aiming it at my chest. I'd just drawn a breath when Clea grabbed the gun, wrestling and hollering, "Mommy, no. Mommy, he's just kidding."

I got up and staggered backward.

"Kidding?" her mother said, trying to yank the gun back. "What kind of kidding do you call that?"

The fingers of both women twisted on the gun. Their hands and faces were scarlet. And Trina's eyes were black. Gaylord backed away now too. I kept jumping around to get out of the firing line.

"Mommy, Duck didn't even know where the goddamn place was."

The gun exploded and the kitchen was instantly dark. Glass and dust rained down on the table from the ceiling globe. The silence lasted so long that I thought somebody must be dead. Then Trina and Clea took turns saying, "Oh God, oh God."

Gaylord went off in the dark and got a lamp from an end table in the living room. He set it in the middle of the kitchen table and plugged the cord into a wall outlet. I got a broom and started sweeping up the glass.

Trina sat in her chair, stiff and staring at the light with a look of astonishment, like it was calling her forth and it was going to demand an accounting of her life.

Gaylord found the dustpan and held it for me to sweep the glass into it.

He said, "Trina, you still want me to do that strip-tease?"

Acknowledgments

My appreciation and thanks go to my editor and publisher Nina Alvarez for her insights, faith, and hard work in shepherding this book through the publishing process. And to my wonderful illustrator, Fawndolyn Valentine.

Many people in recent years have given me encouragement when it was much needed. I especially want to thank James Anderson, Laure-Anne Bosselaar, Sarah Freligh, Betsy Gilbert, Meg Kearney, Tony Leuzzi, Phil Memmer, Martin Naparsteck, and Tanya Whiton.

Grateful acknowledgement goes to the editors of the following publications where these stories first appeared:

"Blissful," in *The Hudson Review*.
"The Zen Adventure of Gerald Riley," in *Shade 2006* (anthology), edited by David Dodd Lee, Four-Way Books.
"Life Is Brief," in *The Solstice Literary Magazine*.
"Air Baggage," in *The Edwin P. Smith Journal*.

ABOUT THE AUTHOR

Steven Huff is the author of a previous collection of stories, *A Pig in Paris* (Big Pencil Press 2008), and three collections of poems: *More Daring Escapes* (Red Hen Press 2008), *The Water We Came From* (FootHills 2003), and *A Fire in the Hill* (Blue Horse Press 2018). He has worked in publishing for many years, and is now founding editor of Tiger Bark Press. He teaches creative writing in the Solstice Low Residency MFA Program at Pine Manor College in Boston, and lives in Rochester, New York.

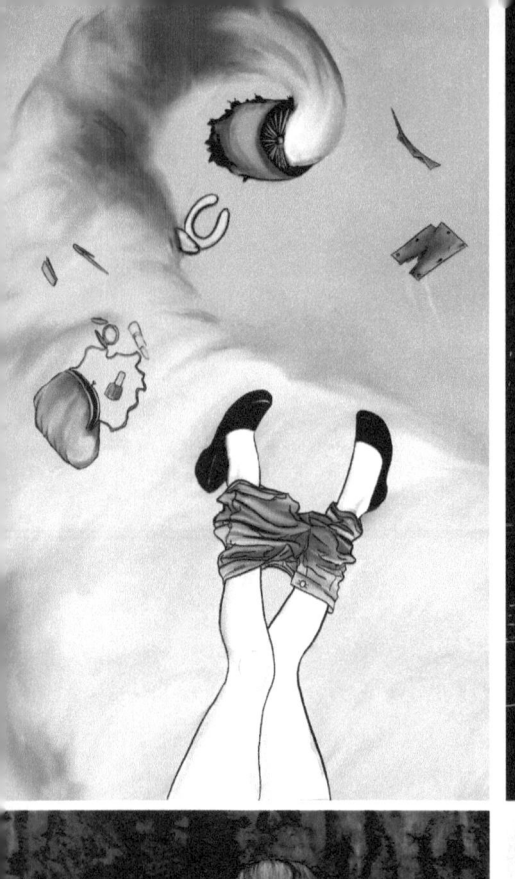

ABOUT THE ARTIST

Fawndolyn Valentine is a classically trained artist living in Rochester, New York.